FROM LEFT TO RIGHT

Music, Murder, Mystery in Washington, D.C.

By
L.C. Goldman

Mountain Valley Publishing, LLC

This is a work of fiction. Names, characters, places and incidents either are the product of the author's imagination or are used fictitiously, and any resemblance to any actual persons, living or dead, events or locales is entirely coincidental.

© Copyright 2008, L.C. Goldman

All Rights Reserved.

No part of this book may be reproduced, stored in a retrieval system, or transmitted by any means, electronic, mechanical, photocopying, recording, or otherwise, without written permission from the author.

ISBN: 978-1-934940-08-2

Other Books by L. C. Goldman

And The Peace Came Tumbling Down

A Big Hit in Pelican Bay

ACKNOWLEDGEMENTS

I dedicate this book to my loving family who encourage, support and offer unconditional love to a man blessed beyond expectations. My children and spouses: Mark and Maureen, Barbara and Larry, Beth and Mark, and Joan.

A special thanks to my gifted and loving grandchildren: Matthew, Emma, Ian, Jared, Lauren, Michael, and Zachary, who light up my life.

"Good afternoon D.C. This is your music man of the airwaves DC, Dancy Carter. It's that time of day to kick back, relax and listen to your favorite artists on your favorite show, "DC ON THE AIR." Right here, Monday thru Friday, 1:00 to 3:00 p.m. on WTOP, 1500 on your AM dial, Washington, D.C.'s number one radio station. Where DC plays the music you ask for, the music you love to hear. But you all know that.

Hope you had a nice lunch and watched those calories. Right? So whether you're at work or lounging in your favorite chair, relax and get in the mood for an exciting two hours of music personally selected by me. And different than anything we've done in the past.

But first let me welcome back from a well-deserved vacation my friend and invaluable producer/engineer, Zack Zoltowsky. Good to have you back Zack. Missed you and your donuts."

"Great to be back, DC. Missed the old music man. Missed the music and chatter. The donuts are coming up at the break."

"Good stuff. But first for you weather buffs, if you're a shut-in or haven't peeked out lately, it's cloudy out there with a chance for rain later this evening or maybe a light snow dusting, if the now 36 degree temperature continues dropping like a brick out of a 30-story window. Almost 15 degrees in just the last hour.

No need to despair, folks, cause DC won't leave you out in the cold. From 1-3 p.m., right here on WTOP 1500 on your AM dial, I'm going to warm up your ears and heart with a musical tribute to the storied African-American artists who not only broke the color barrier in the music world, but made Jazz America's one and only true musical genre. All Jazz royalty.

A Count, Count Basie. A Duke, Duke Ellington. An Earl, Earl "Fatha" Hines. A King, Nat "King" Cole. And an Ambassador to the world, Louis "Satchmo" Armstrong. And rest assured all the ladies out there, I haven't forgotten you. No way. My first segment features another royal, the First Lady Day, Billie Holiday, to those of you who didn't know they were one and the same.

But here's another surprise. It's a different format today. Not just one artist following another, but two hours broken up into 15-minute segments featuring each performer. What's more, to further your uninterrupted listening enjoyment, DC is going to give you more music with less commercials.

Nice idea, eh, Zack?"

"Great stuff, DC. Wish I'd thought of it. Can't wait."

"However, there is one little accommodation I had to make to the bottom-line suits who run this station. Only one commercial will run in each segment. A small price to pay, folks.

One other really small thing you can do for DC. Pick up one of the fine products advertised throughout the program at your favorite store. I'll be happy. My bosses ecstatic. The store owners overjoyed. And the sponsors grateful enough to advertise again.

Enough talk. Let's get with the Jazz, right Zack?"

"Right DC. Right on and ready to roll."

"Keep it right here, you hear. "DC ON THE AIR" on WTOP 1500 on your AM dial. We'll be back in 60 seconds with Billie Holiday."

Fancy Dancy Carter, DC to radio music fans all over the D.C. area, is the music man of the Washington airwaves. His patter and chatter always amusing and informative. His platter selection embraces the great artists of Jazz, Pop, Swing and the Blues. The golden oldies that have thrilled generations. DC knows the genesis of every record he plays. When it was recorded. Where. Who were the side men backing up the featured artist, the celebrated instrumentalists. Even stories that took place at the recording studio, the live feed from a hotel ballroom or theater. The story behind the story.

"DC ON THE AIR" is the number one program in Washington, D.C. Music at its best. Controversial as well. He is a liberal gadfly who champions every liberal cause and makes his views stridently known. This incurs the wrath of right wing politicians, leaders of conservative causes and listeners who love his music selection, but hate his point of view. And often disagree. They phone in to challenge that point of view, taking him to task for his liberal bent.

It is the only music program that sometimes resembles a talk radio call-in forum. It's DC against the D.C. establishment, against the D.C. radical fringe. And he loves every minute of it. So do a vast legion of listeners. Those who believe he can do no wrong, say no wrong.

He is by far and away the Washington celebrity with as much celebrity as any politico or high profile person in town.

Who is this articulate, aggressive personality who has captured the ears, the minds of all Washingtonians? The man who has taken on Republicans, Democrats...anyone whose ideology doesn't jibe with his.

Dancy Carter was born in a small town in South Dakota and worked his way through menial disc jockey jobs all over the Midwest. With his eye on the sparrow, he gravitated to the nation's capitol, and used his vast musical knowledge and engaging personality to get his own program. In two years, "DC ON THE AIR" gave Dancy Carter his forum to win over Washington, D.C. And with incredible self-promotion, Dancy Carter, now more commonly known as DC, became the musical guru, the voice of D. C.

DC is tall, affable and handsome in a rugged way, with a distinctive white streak running through a thick head of black hair. A natural occurrence I might add. His smooth delivery, and well modulated speech pattern delivered in a whiskey-throated, somewhat husky voice gave him the title of "The Voice That Soothes." Women fell in love with the sound, and men sought to duplicate it. Always impeccably groomed in bespoke English custom-tailored suits, shirts, ties and shoes, he was the number one choice to speak at colleges to adoring audiences, various charity functions, and even the hallowed halls of Congress to a committee of the House of Representatives holding hearings on the effects of gangsta rap on the mores of young people.

If there was a cause, DC was out front, raising dollars and awareness. Liberal causes, that is. He was the ultimate liberal wearing that label on the sleeve of his $2000 suit.

"DC ON THE AIR" was on most Washingtonians' listen-to-list, even if you didn't buy into his ideology. 1 p.m. Monday to Friday for two hours was DC time in offices, college dorms and households in the Washington area and its environs. The ratings were huge, with no other station even close. His following loyal. His adversaries confrontational, but very attentive. Sponsors renewed contracts immediately and there was a long list of those waiting to place advertising dollars into the show.

All in all two great hours of radio. Two hours that were completely sold 52 weeks a year. And two profitable hours for the man from a little town in South Dakota: The highest paid DJ in D.C., maybe the country, with the wardrobe, deluxe apartment and life style to show for it.

"Hey Zack, cue up the nigga lady's first cut, Body & Soul."

"What? Did I hear you right? If so, that's no way to talk about the lady. The lady you say you revere. I hope your mike is closed or that liberal masquerade you hide behind will be shattered in a heartbeat."

"It's closed."

"That's good, Mr. Bigot. Don't believe you. I'm just back and you're starting that stuff again."

"What stuff?"

"That trash talk. It's not very becoming. And I hope to God that's not you Dancy Carter. Or is it?"

"Bigot? Are you kidding? It's me Zacko. Champion of the people. For the people. Just pulling your proverbial leg, Mr. Sensitive Producer. Would it be less offensive if I said schvartze. Would your Jewish ears accept that? Eh!"

"Don't play that game with me, DC . There's no difference. An ethnic slur is an ethnic slur. And I don't think for one minute that you were pulling my leg in gutter talk or in Yiddish. What's going on? You used to take umbrage at any racial slur. What changed?"

"Nothing's changed, my Hebrew friend. You've just lost your sense of humor. I sort of kvell, if that's the right yiddishism, seeing your knee-jerk reaction when I'm funning around. You're no different than those right wingers that call in and twist everything I say about some liberal cause."

"That's not the same thing, DC. Now you're twisting the truth. And if you're funning, well it's not funny."

"Oh, come on, Zacko. Get off your high horse. You know me. The real me for more than three years now. The DC with a real love for my black brothers and sisters, not to mention all the Jews in my life.

Besides that, you know I sing at that black Baptist church on many a Sunday. Love that gospel/hallelujah stuff. And did you forget my attending those Saturday Bar Mitzvahs at your shul?

Bigot? Not me my friend. Not me. No way. Just pushing your button. And you know what, I think I've succeeded."

"What's this black brother and sister crap? The only gospel you ever sing is the one about DC. And shul? You go alright, but always seem to get there in time for the bagels and cream cheese when services are over. And to play kissy-face with the gals in the sisterhood.

Face it, my celebrity friend, you're a pseudo-liberal wearing a mask that hides your lily-white, Methodist, anti-everything face. I've just realized it, and you knew it all the time. There's no family involved. You're a one man family by yourself. I hope you treat your black lady friend with more respect than you gave Billie Holiday. I like you DC, as if my job depended on it. And I hope I still have a job after all this. No matter what, please go back to being the politically correct DC that I used to admire."

"That's getting a load off your mind, friend. Honest too. Respect you for that. But one thing is sure. I know how to get under your skin, Zacko. Don't I?"

"Sure, you do..."

"Uh, uh don't go there again my 'loyal, honest' friend. It's starting to wear thin. Okay? Your job is safe, but the discussion is over. Enough of the racial/ethnic stuff. The clock is ticking down and it's time to get some Body & Soul music on the air. Wheel the reel, Zacko. Cut it for a twenty second intro to Lady Day. Watch my hand signal. Thank you."

"Right you are, oh leader of righteous men."

"Ah, that's more like it, Mr. Producer."

That's the way it's been for the last six months. DC and Zack sparring between commercial breaks. Zack would be on DC's case for his veiled, if not direct, bigoted remarks about African-Americans, Jews, Italians, Irish and Hispanics. In Zack's mind DC was an equal opportunity bigot, if not an outright racist.

Suffice it to say, that's not the way Dancy Carter saw himself. He was funning. Pulling Zack's leg. Getting under his skin. Getting a rise out of him. Pushing his buttons because he took himself so seriously, and DC got a rise out of torturing him. Maybe because he felt superior. He was the man. The celebrity. The boss of his show, with absolute control. Zack was just a lackey.

Their discussion always ended with DC getting in the last words. Professing his love and affection for everyone. Not a bigoted bone in his body.

And that's how his vast listening audience, broadcast colleagues, friends and the hundreds of people connected with the causes he championed viewed Dancy Carter.

On the air he crossed swords with the radical right. Never yielding to taunts about his liberal leanings. Off the air he was in the forefront of many causes. He marched in protest parades for black rights, Hispanic rights. Raised untold thousands of dollars to fight anti-Semitism or anti-anything. Served as a board member of the Anti-Defamation League for Jews and Italians. Championed gay pride against the homophobic fringe. If there was a liberal cause, DC was the rebel that manned the hustings against the evil of bigotry.

So who was the real Dancy Carter? The do-gooder or the no-gooder? Why the voice of bigotry in the studio with the mike off, the pointed jabs at every ethnic group in his repartee with Zack Zoltowsky?

Good question, Zack often pondered. Was there some dark side to his overinflated ego that wouldn't, couldn't let the sunshine in? Or was he merely joking, funning as DC put it. More important, why? Zack spent many a restless night mulling over these questions. How could he turn it on and off without feeling at least a twinge of guilt or remorse? It was puzzling to say the least. DC certainly was a man full of contradictions. Complex for sure. A paradox bordering on an enigma. Yet it may be the guiding force that transcends his being just a DJ radio music man and one who has Washington, D.C. eating out of the palm of his hand.

The haunting sounds of Billie Holiday's Body and Soul brought Zack out of his funk about the guy who put bread on his table. Now he was back in his real world of engineer and producer. Back in the world of music. The world he loved with a passion. The reason he took the job with the impresario of radio. And a world he had better not jeopardize by putting DC's feet to the fire of racism. It could send his world up in flames.

Billie Holiday's incredible, one-of-a-kind, soulful sound was caressing every nook and cranny of the small studio inhabited by DC and Zack. Sitting so close to the great one, Zack was fascinated by DC's reaction to the lady he just blasphemed. He was sitting back in his easy chair, headset on the console, hands clasped behind his head, his eyes closed. A beatific smile lit up his face, enrapt with every note, every word, every phrased nuance by the unchallenged diva of Jazz.

It was times like this that Zack felt DC was the man he always thought he was. A man without prejudice or racial and ethnic bias. A man for the people. All the people. A man whom a higher authority had destined to be the champion of every cause, all the downtrodden, all the disenfranchised.

He prayed that he was right.

"DC back with you folks. How about that foot-stomping stuff? That was One O'clock Jump by Bill Basie, the Count from Red Bank, New Jersey and his jumping big band. A great group with Lester Young and Illinois Jacquet on tenor sax, Buck Clayton and Harry "Sweets" Edison on trumpet, Freddie Green on guitar, the master Jo Jones on drums, and of course, the inimitable Mr. Basie on the 88's.

Sorry to say, but that brings us to that time of day when the little hand of the clock is on the three and big one nearing twelve. The end of my day with you. Hope you enjoyed our musical journey with our tribute to royalty...the great African-American Jazz artists.

Tomorrow, another musical surprise. Another starset program featuring the many different styles of icons of Italian-American descent: Francis Albert Sinatra, Dean Martin, Vic Damone, Jerry Vale, Al Martino, Jimmy Rosselli and the great Tony Bennett.

So when tomorrow rolls around and the little hand is on the one and the big one is on the twelve, tune In to "DC ON THE AIR" right here on WTOP, 1500 on your AM dial. I'm Dancy Carter, DC to one and all. Enjoy the rest of your afternoon all you wonderful people in D.C.

Zack, take us out with another great Basie arrangement, "April in Paris." And oh yeah, see you later Mrs. B."

"Good show DC. I enjoyed it as much as your listeners."

"Thanks, Zacko. It was more than good. That was great stuff. My kind of music. My kind of artists. My kind of people. I only hope that my white audience dug the artistry and incredible musicianship of those marvelous black performers."

"No question in my mind. You sure know your stuff. All that info about each song, that I'm sure few knew about. The sidemen. Where it was recorded. What year. What record label. That was DC at his best. Your inimitable style. They couldn't help but love every minute of it."

"Nice words, Mr. Producer. But kudos to you, too. You hit every cue on the nose. Made my segues sharp and made me sound good. Better than good. If I haven't mentioned it lately, we make a great team."

"Yeah, yeah, DC, a great team. Equals, right?"

"Right you are Zacko."

"Wrong, DC. Maybe in the booth, but remember you get the big bucks and I get the leavings. Not so equal.

How about that raise you promised me four months ago? Sure could use it."

"Well, we can't rush important financial considerations, can we? Hold your water, buddy, just pulling your leg again. Funning. Tomorrow I'll speak to the head Jew and threaten to reveal he eats pork on the high holidays."

"You bigot."

"Bye, bye Zack. See you Monday."

"Have a good weekend, DC. Try to make shul tomorrow. It's Bar Mitzvah time and they'll be having lots of lox with those bagels and cream cheese."

"Fantastic. That's my favorite Jew food."

The bar at Dukes, Washington's favorite watering hole and restaurant was its usual frenetic place. Three deep at each bar stool. People lined up four abreast in front of the hostess waiting for a table. Many with a twenty dollar bill in hand waving it to get the maitre'd's attention. A table was hard to come by without a reservation, so flashing of the green was a way to get one's name moved up the list. Especially for the out-of-towners. The noise was deafening. Perfect, however, for those private, often secret and whispered conversations between Senators, lobbyists, ad men, PR honchos, not to mention married men putting the moves on interns with well-rehearsed sweet nothings into very impressionable ears. Dukes was the place for the ordinary man or woman to make the scene, to be seen, or to see important Washingtonians.

In a secluded, dim-lit corner table, where a flashlight was needed to read the menu, sat Dancy Carter. His private table in his home away from home. His black lady friend nowhere to be seen. The vision in pink sitting across from him was the very blond, very beautiful Jennifer Cabot, granddaughter of the powerful Mr. Cabot from Boston. (Remember the Cabots and Lodges?)

Jennifer Cabot had breeding written all over her. The family name, a listing in the social register, an ivy league education, and a multi-million dollar bank account courtesy of a trust fund set up by her late, lamented father.

She came to Washington, D.C. after being graduated Summa Cum Laude from Harvard with an eye towards carving out a political career, either as a staff aide to the Senator from Massachusetts or as a lobbyist on environmental issues. Mama Cabot, doyenne of Boston society, wrote the letters of introduction (a euphemism for give my daughter a job) and made the necessary phone calls. However, she was determined to make it on her own and walked away from Mama's sphere of influence. She used her brains, beauty and family name to land a job selling ads at radio station

WTOP. Within a short time she became the number one time salesperson at the station and six months later, this aggressive, motivated, highly ambitious debutante's debutant attained the lofty position of V.P. of Administration. Dancy Carter's boss lady.

All this was easy for Jennifer Cabot and expected by her. Growing up as a Cabot certainly had its advantages and Jennifer learned at an early age the power of the Cabot name. The world became her oyster. A pearl in every shell. There were Cotillion balls where being crowned queen was a given. Debutante coming out parties where more often than not she outshone the coming out Deb, transatlantic cruises, summers in the south of France, hobnobbing with Boston's snobbish elite. Nothing was ever denied this young beauty of privilege. She played the field of all the eligible bachelors, scions of the rich and famous, and left them in her wake. But play was all she did. Whatever Jennifer wanted, Jennifer got.

Her first exposure to the real world of the dating game, to the reality of being denied was coming face to face with Dancy Carter. She wanted him badly, but her not so subtle advances were rejected, much less not even acknowledged. She tried. Oh, how she tried, using all the wiles, all the feminine tricks she honed in the social world of Boston. Nothing seemed to puncture the armor of Dancy Carter.

She invited him to gala parties at her mother's 20 room mansion in Georgetown, where the guest list consisted of Washington glitterati, political VIP's, corporate CEOs, Ambassadors from countries small and large.

DC never showed.

Then there were the private dinner parties with a select A-list few: Billionaires, movie stars, Senators, Congressmen, a poet laureate and famous writers, Kennedy Center honorees. One time the Vice President dropped in for dessert.

Dancy never showed.

To add insult to injury he never even responded to her RSVP invitations. Jennifer Cabot was totally frustrated at her inability to make him out. Hissy angry that she couldn't make out with him.

It was something Jennifer Cabot never experienced when she was on the scent. An ego deflator to say the least. A slap in the face to the Princess of Boston elite. A royal miss used to getting her way with men. Men who could buy and sell Dancy Carter.

Dancy not only didn't bow to her Royal Highness, he never even acknowledged she existed. Imagine a Cabot being dismissed by nothing more than a radio disc jockey. It was time she put this arrogant, self-important, socially rude person in his place.

Indeed.

She initiated staff meetings for all on-air personalities, producers and salesmen. Mandatory that all attend. She was determined to bring to bear all her executive powers to bring Dancy Carter to heel. It had little or no effect. DC rarely, if ever, attended any staff meeting or company party. He was a power to himself and meetings and parties were just a waste of his time.

Jennifer was furious. Rejection to her social soirees was one thing, ignoring her executive position, her authority at the station was quite another. She snapped off a stinging interoffice memo, countersigned by the station owner, demanding that he attend these meetings. With venom etched in every word, she reminded the high and mighty Carter that all meetings required his attendance. Read clause #3 in his contract. Be there were her last words.

DC got the not so subtle message and began to attend some meetings. When he did he was the center of attraction. Staff members fell all over themselves to have a few minutes of his time. Especially the females. Dancy Carter was his usual affable, animated self with everyone, especially the ladies, but virtually ignored the lady from Boston. When he did respond to a question from her he answered in monosyllables. Aloof and rather cold. Miss V.P. of Administration was beside herself that control of the meeting was being undermined by a man without breeding...just a guy who played music. She tried to keep her inner rage in check, but only felt subservient in the company of the man whose pay checks she signed.

After one meeting, DC seemed to relent a bit. His first hello to her came when he said goodbye. But this time Jennifer was willing to accept any sign that the ice was breaking. That the cool air was warming. She felt a glimmer of encouragement. Not just because of his hello, but what she saw in his eyes. They never left hers. She had seen this kind of eye contact many times before with men that had eyes for her. Her feminine instincts proved right on. At the next meeting, DC waited until everyone left the room and in a smug, almost brusque manner invited her to have dinner with him at Dukes. Jennifer was elated, but kept her bubbling emotions in check. This was Mohammed coming to the Mountain. She was aware that not every woman received a dinner invitation to his private drinking and eating refuge. His home away from home. Being in the public eye, DC often opted for a private dinner at Dukes. Many times alone. Alone at his private table in and out of the way corner, where the light was dim and the autograph hounds were out of bounds.

Jennifer Cabot almost said yes before "at Dukes" left his lips.

After the waiter took their drink order, Jennifer couldn't resist putting DC's feet to the fire about their cool relationship. Their non-relationship.

"Well, Mr. Carter, why your sudden change of heart after turning down all my invitations? Was it something I said? Or did? Or are you just lonely for female company because your favorite chocolate cookie is away for the weekend?"

The chocolate cookie taunt brought a slight smile to his ruggedly handsome face, which brought a broad grin to hers.

"Low blow, Miss Cabot, really low."

"Don't interrupt, Mr. Carter. Not finished. In fact I'm just getting started."

She rambled on for over five minutes. Question after question, hardly stopping to take a breath. Almost as if she didn't want answers. Or anything negative.

DC seemed distracted by this barrage of questions, but managed to listen attentively. This was foreign territory for him, since no woman ever attacked him in this fashion. All he could do was stare at her. Stare into those gleaming, big-as-saucers, green eyes. Barely blinking his own. Although the multitude of questions and the monotony of her voice was starting to annoy him, he only had eyes for those deep, penetrating green eyes. Much less her beautifully heart-shaped mouth with those subtly colored red lips. And then there were those sparkling white teeth. Perfectly aligned. Probably cost Mama Cabot a lot of green stuff to give her those 32 sparkling whites.

All in all he was overwhelmed with the fact that the rich and socially advantaged Jennifer Cabot had a face that would make an ordinary man walk through fire to plant a kiss on those inviting lips. Finally after what seemed an eternity, DC reached out and brushed her lips with his fingers, then placed his fingers on his own lips, convincingly suggesting that her question period was over.

Jennifer stopped talking in mid-sentence, shivering with anticipation at his touch.

"Miss Cabot, stop talking and start listening to me. Please."

"Why?" she whispered, barely able to breathe. "Am I boring you?"

"No Miss Chatterbox, not boring at all, but now it's my turn to ask questions and I promise to wait for your answers."

The very way he said it, with his impeccable enunciation and that incredibly throaty voice, gave her the feeling she was participating in a sexual experience. Orgasmic to say the least.

"Ask on, Mr. Music Man. I'm all ears. What do you have in mind?"

"Mundane questions."

"Mundane? Tell me, Mr. Carter, what kind of mundane questions do you have in mind?"

"Things I want to know about you. How you think. What do you think about? Unfortunately, I left the complete list in my office, so I'll do the best from memory."

"Funny. Funny. That's the one thing I know about you."

"First, however, the answer to your question about my chocolate cookie. Which I took to be an obvious attempt to stick a needle into my overinflated ego of a balloon."

"Sorry about that."

"No need to be. The truth is she's back at my apartment where she should be, cooking, cleaning and ironing my shirts. Satisfied?"

"Touché Mr. Carter," as the redness crept into her face. "That's really funny."

"How old are you, Miss Cabot?"

"But why my age?"

"Forgive me dear Jennifer, but please don't answer a question with a question. That's a Jewish trait unbecoming to a Wasp."

"Ask the question again, DC."

"Please tell me your age."

"Old enough not to be considered jail bait."

"Jennifer, Jennifer! Your age."

"Twenty three next week."

"Happy Birthday. Who did you vote for in the last Presidential election?"

"Isn't that supposed to be a personal, private right, known only to the one voting?"

"There you go again, answering a question with a question. Are you sure you're not Jewish? Once again. Who?"

"The Republican, alright. Does that put me on the wrong side of your Democratic leaning ?"

"Why the Republican?"

"That's easy. I'm a Cabot and the Cabots have voted Republican probably since the Republic was formed. Many had the privilege of serving under Republican Presidents. What's more we stand for all the values and ideals I have always been taught."

"Since the Republic was formed?"

"Oh, you know what I mean."

"Understood. What values and ideals?"

"Lower taxes, less government. Pro life. A strong military, etc., etc."

"Do you really independently care about those issues or is your vote pre-ordained, handed down from generation to generation? Or worse yet, are you merely mouthing the Republican platform without real conviction?"

"Never gave it much thought. But if that's your way of saying I'm an airhead, influenced by family tradition and not independent thinking…if that's where you're going, you're wrong. Dead wrong. You don't have a clue who and what I am."

"Maybe not, but have you ever taken your so-called independent convictions to the streets? And I don't mean Wall Street."

"What street do you mean?"

"The pavement, dear Jennifer. Marching in a protest parade against busing, or blacks getting preferential treatment for college, or that welfare should be abolished and people get jobs instead of being on the government dole."

"Well, I—"

"Have you ever sat in a sit-in at an abortion clinic lobbying to have Roe v. Wade overturned?"

"No, Mr. Carter. No way. Cabots don't march in the street protesting anything. We do it our own way, the right way. The way the democratic process is supposed to work. Working through our elected representatives in Congress. Through the voting process. But if you must know, I did sign a petition against abortions in my sophomore year at Harvard."

"My, my. That much conviction, eh. That's a far cry from conviction, Miss Cabot. I would call that standing on the sidelines and hoping others take care of your convictions."

"That's unfair. I did what I had to do then and I do what I have to do now. In my own way."

"What way is that?"

"We support candidates—"

"Support? I guess that means that Mama Cabot, you and other members of the family throw a lot of those Cabot dollars around to guarantee that their people win."

"What's wrong with that? We feel that's the civilized way to get good government. Certainly not your way which is civil disobedience. Is that less conviction?"

"Oh, so you buy good government. Sorry about that."

"That's not fair, and you should feel sorry for saying it."

"Ok, let's move on. How do you feel about blacks, Jews, Hispanics, illegal immigrants, any ethnic group? Any animosity or prejudice?"

"No. No animosity. I don't dislike any of them. I just don't socialize with any of them. That's my right, right? I can choose my friends without you thinking I'm prejudiced."

"I see. You don't hang out with 'them'. Is that because they are inferior to you?"

"That's not what I mean. You're twisting my words."

"Okay, let's untwist them. Has a black man ever been invited to one of your A-list dinners? And I don't count the ones serving the canapés."

Getting a bit irritated, Jennifer Cabot straightened up in her chair and through clenched teeth said, "Stop DC. Stop right here. I'm at a loss to know where you are going with this."

"Just to get to know your political mindset."

"Forgive me, but I thought we were having dinner to get to know each other better. Or that's what I thought you had in mind."

"That's what I did have in mind."

"Well you could have fooled me, music man. No politics, okay. Let's just enjoy each other's company in this secluded, romantically dim-lit corner. And I place the emphasis on romantic."

"I'll try."

"Good. Then cut the crap about my prejudices. If I have some, so what? I won't admit to anything knowing your ultra liberal views on causes I'm familiar with and those I never heard about. My instincts tell me you're probing for a reason. Maybe any reason to fend off my obvious advances to you."

"I wasn't aware of the obvious."

"Obviously, you're a very good liar, too. For the record, I am being obvious. Very much so. But my politics, my prejudices, my choice of friends have nothing to do with my sexual desires. Republicans, even bigoted ones, enjoy sex."

"Is that what you think, Jennifer? That plumbing your political and racial state of mind would be a turn-off to sleep with someone who is ideologically to the right of me?"

"That's exactly what I think."

"No beautiful lady. A better, more logical reason would be not to have an affair with someone in the office. Better still not to sleep with the boss lady."

"Well, what am I to think? Is all your questioning some kind of test? Are you trying to convert me and hopefully recruit me for some of your liberal causes? Then sleeping with the boss lady would be okay."

"Not for one single moment. You are a beautiful, desirable woman. Even more so in this dim light. Especially when you get ticked off. Any red-blooded left or right winger would kill to get you into bed. And for the record, I wouldn't think of trying to convert you or use you to march in the streets. Those high heels would kill your feet. Big blisters or corns."

"Funny, music man. Disingenuous, too. Your reputation precedes you."

"Reputation? Is that just women in general or my chocolate cookie?"

"Women and your chocolate cookie I can compete with. Your politics pose a bigger challenge. We probably would be at each other's throats about some issue, ethnic or ideology, minutes after we made love."

"So that's it. I think you're a right wing fanatic and you think I'm a dyed-in-the-wool, flaming liberal that detests being in the same room with anyone who doesn't share my liberal views. Now that's a surprise, don't you think?"

"I'm surprised, DC, that you are surprised that I should be surprised that I've come to that conclusion. One doesn't have to be a Mensa candidate to draw the inference."

"But you are a Mensa."

"Don't be cute. Remember I monitor your show every day. I love the music and the chatter, and am completely astounded at the loyalty of your audience. That's not the problem."

"What is?"

"Being unfair in your monologues and interviews with guests who have opposite points of view."

"It's my show, lady, and I have the right to play the music I play and to say what I want to say."

"Only to a point. There is a regulatory standard of fairness at the FCC. It has nothing to do with the music. You don't have to play a Rock N' Roll song every time you play one of your jazz favorites."

"Rock N' Roll?"

"Don't interrupt. Political opinion is a different turn of the turntable. WTOP, you, have to give equal time to all political points of view, to all candidates during election time, to guests who disagree. And be fair, too. You host a music show not a political opinion forum."

"I get the big audience because I'm both."

"Not in their eyes. The FCC bureaucrats are supersensitive about fairness and can create problems for us when license renewal time comes up. In their view, 'DC ON THE AIR' hasn't complied. Management, including me, has a responsibility to its shareholders, much less the public, to protect the franchise."

"I had no idea that the FCC had such a doctrine. But who's to protect my listeners from the politicos who don't have their best interest in mind?"

"Irrelevant, DC."

"Not to me, dear lady. So monitor all you want. I will continue to air my views, liberal as that may be, until my listeners tell me otherwise."

"That won't cut it, DC."

"Maybe not, but I'll leave it to you to take care of that equal time stuff."

Dancy looked squarely into those green eyes and slowly said, "I will welcome those who disagree with me with open arms and an open mike. Fair enough?"

"Only if you are fair, Mr. Carter."

"Alright. Now that we've beaten all these issues to death, let's cut out the fencing and dancing. For the last time, converting you never entered my mind. I wish it did. You'd make a beautiful liberal. With that confession to concession, it's time to declare a truce and get to the real issue."

"Which is, Mr. Carter?"

"Are you hungry?"

"Hungry? I'm starved and a little drunk as well. I was wondering if food was ever on the political menu. I suspected that you were trying to wear me down with a starvation diet of causes."

"Almost, dear Jennifer. Dukes is just the place for politicians to sell their ideology with alcohol du jour. However the food is far better than the political palaver. So let's eat, okay? If you don't think I'm being a bit chauvinistic, may I do the ordering?"

"Gallant, DC. Extremely gallant. That's the way Republican men in my family do it."

"Alright, I'll be a Republican for tonight. We'll start with the Jumbo Crab Meat Cocktail. Really superb. Concocted from Maryland's finest blue crab meat. Almost nothing added. And if you like Prime Rib, the chef served an apprenticeship at L'Ecole Prime Rib Cooking Society, learning from master chefs to roast the meat to mouth-watering perfection."

"Tell me you didn't make that up, DC."

"Just a bit."

"Whatever. Sounds good enough to eat."

"And for the pièce de resistance, the wine will be a favorite of mine, the 1959 Chateau Petrus. If that suits your palate."

"Just perfect, Monsieur Carter. I might add that's the house wine of the Cabots."

"I had that feeling, Mlle Cabot. Michael, we're ready to order. No menu. The lady has agreed to the specialties of the house. Merci."

"Good, good morning, Zack."

"Hi, DC. Why the big smile?"

"Is it that big? Well there's a very good reason. I think I'm in love."

"With yourself, no doubt."

"No funning, Mr. Doubter. It's with a real live girl."

"Congratulations. Did you finally tell Miss Black America how you feel about her?"

"She's not the one."

"You broke up? What happened?"

"No breakup, yet, but I think I've found a soulmate who's the opposite of me politically. And you know what? I love it."

"I think I heard it someplace, DC, that opposites attract. Anybody I know?"

"It's on a need to know basis, Mr. Producer, and you don't need to know. Unwrinkle your brow, my friend, you'll be the first to know when I want it to be known. Might even announce it on the show."

"Wow, the great Dancy Carter in love. I'm honored that you even told me that much. However, not to change the lovely subject, but we have a show to do. Get your headset ready and get your head into today's program. Thirty minutes to air. What are we playing?"

"Love songs, Zack. The heart-stopping ones by Gershwin, Porter, Kern, and Rogers and Hammerstein. All that dreamy stuff. I want to travel on a musical cloud of love and let my listeners get that feeling, too. Let's open with Sinatra doing Sammy Cahn's "'Love is Better the Second Time Around'."

"That bad, eh, DC?"

"Yeah, that bad and more."

" By the way does our mystery lady know how you feel?"

"Not yet, but I think I know how she feels."

"What else would I expect or think, DC? I only hope she's not just another notch in your love belt."

"Not this time, Mr. Naysayer. Get some CDs ready."

"11 minutes to air. Oh, I almost forgot that boss lady Cabot called to tell you that she's booked Congressman Barlow for an interview at the two o'clock break. She said you'll understand."

"I do. It's my commentary about pro-choice that brings Barlow to my mike."

"I'm not sure I get it. Isn't that Barlow guy a rabid pro-lifer?"

"And more. Blame it on the FCC."

"What the hell does that mean?"

"It means the suits here are sucking up to the bureaucrats at the Federal Communications Commission to comply with some fairness doctrine. Equal time nonsense. License renewal is the real issue."

"Is this new to you, DC? I've never known you to be fair to an opposite point of view. Why the change?"

"Getting soft, Zack. Have to play by the rules. Orders from the boss lady. The rules, Zacko, or those big bucks they pay us might be gone with the wind.

Let's not dwell on unpleasantries today. Cue Sinatra, Maestro. It's heading towards the hour."

"Watch for my signal, DC. Five four, three, two one, and take it."

"Good afternoon, D.C., this is your music man of the airwaves, DC, Dancy Carter. Time again for 'DC ON THE AIR', Monday through Friday 1 to 3 PM on WTOP, 1500 AM, Washington's number one radio station. But you all know that.

It's a balmy day out there, a comfortable 65 degrees, just a few clouds and old King Sol brightening up a gorgeous blue sky. So sit back and smell the roses folks, 'cause love is in the air. Go ahead and tell someone you love him or her or fall in love all over again.

Yes, good friends, for the next two hours you're going to hear all about love as messrs Gershwin, Porter, Kern, Rogers and Hammerstein and others put those lovely words to their music.

Francis Albert sets the mood with a favorite of mine, 'Love is Better the Second Time Around.' Billie May provides the backdrop.

It's all yours, Mr. Producer."

"Jennifer, it's DC."

"You don't say, as if I didn't recognize the mellifluous tones of Dancy Carter. What's up?"

"Did you hear the Barlow segment?"

"I was all ears."

"So was I fair enough?"

"Barely fair. You really didn't have to tell him that his misdirected and misguided views on abortion will turn off his state's women electorate when he decides to run again."

"Well, I had to be me, no?" It wouldn't be 'DC ON THE AIR' if I softballed a prejudiced, rabid pro-life pol like Barlow. What would my loyal, trusting listeners think?"

"I couldn't care less what they think. Only what the FCC thinks."

"You should care what they think. Don't forget ratings. That brings in the big bucks, boss lady."

"Don't change the subject, DC. Think about tomorrow."

"What happens then?"

"Senator Harris is your guest to talk about defense spending and rebut your tirade today."

"Harris? He's the top hawk in the Senate, and would attack Iran or Syria tomorrow if it was up to him."

"Don't attack back, DC. Remember to play fair."

"I can't play the dove or back down to him or his inflated defense appropriation bill."

"You don't have to be a dove, love. Just say your piece without any rancor, without bashing what he says. Agree to disagree, and let your listeners draw their own conclusions. That's fairness. That's equal time for controversial issues, DC."

"I'm not too sure that's fair for my audience."

"Don't care, DC. That's what the government watchdogs want to hear. That keeps our license in good standing. More important, that keeps me signing your exorbitant paychecks."

"Well when my pocketbook is threatened, I guess I have to fall in line. Even if I don't like it."

"Trust me, DC, you'll learn to like it."

"How long, Jen?"

"How long, what?"

"How long are you going to send these hack politicians over to my show to air their unpalatable opinions?"

"Until our license is renewed. And then according to how I feel."

"That's Jim Dandy. It won't make sleeping at night any easier."

"Speaking of tonight, DC, will I see you?"

"Got a slight scheduling problem. Promised I'd have a pizza and watch a movie at home with the chocolate cookie."

"Oh! Don't forget to take Pepcid AC, DC, before chomping on the pizza. Try to keep your zipper closed, too."

"Now, now, no petulance, Boston lady. I'll try and get out of it. Call you later. Wait, don't hang up. I'm getting out of it now. Where do we meet?"

"My place, lover boy. Candlelight and all. I bought a couple of bottles of the Cabot's house wine."

"You read me like a book. I'll bring the music and flowers."

"Got the flowers, just bring the music. Ravel, right?"

"By the way, did you like my all-love-song segments today? It was dedicated to you. I had Zack pick those songs with you in mind."

"Nice. Especially the Gershwin part. Otherwise a tad bland. Now, Ravel's Bolero, that always gets my blood boiling. See you at 7:30."

DC couldn't believe he was so nervous. It's not like he'd never been to a woman's apartment before. Yet this was different. Love not lust was in his heart. To work off the nervous energy he passed up the elevator and walked the four flights to Jennifer Cabot's duplex apartment in the infamous Watergate complex.

When he rang the bell, Jennifer yelled out, "The door is open, DC. Make yourself comfortable. Just getting decent. Be out in a jiffy."

He couldn't believe his eyes. Opulence surrounded him wherever he looked or turned. Picasso's and Renoir's on every wall. A beautiful antique Dutch hutch was the centerpiece of the living room. The velvet sofas looked like they had never been sat on. The Louis XIV dining room chairs were in pristine condition.

The track lighting was turned down low. The fireplace in full blaze cast an eerie, seductive light in the room. The dining room table was set with exquisite sterling silverware, fine china and damask napkins.

Candles of various sizes were flickering on the coffee table and mantle. There was a delightful aroma of cinnamon essence that permeated every nook and cranny.

The rich certainly are different, he thought. This was an apartment probably decorated and furnished by one of America's leading interior decorators, and surely not paid on the installment plan. This wasn't the living quarters of a V.P. of Administration at a local AM radio station. Not with her salary. This was Boston society money, old money, creating an environment that Architectural Digest would feature.

He was still standing in complete awe when she ambled into the living room clad in a skimpy, but breathtaking Scaaisi dressing gown, one strap removed from being a negligee.

"Why are you standing, DC? Sit down. That lounge chair is really for lounging."

"My, my, you, the gown look beautiful. The designer must have designed it just for you."

"Hardly. Please sit. How do you like my humble abode?"

"I'm humbled. Where's the phone? I have to cancel the Domino pizza I ordered with what's probably on your menu this evening."

"Yep. No need to duplicate the extra large one, with extra pepperoni that's simmering in the oven. Did you bring Ravel?"

"Yes ma'am. The long playing version by the Boston Pops. Felt that was politically correct, geographically speaking."

"That's why they call you the 'music man' of D.C., DC. You think of little things like that. For starters, pour the wine while I set the CD up and check on the pizza. Try not to spill a drop. At $250 a bottle, a drop amounts to quite a lot of money."

"My, my, the poor little rich girl has a miser's mentality."

"Got to on my miserly salary. How about that Ravel? What passion."

"Right. Lots of passion."

"How about a toast, Carter?"

"What'll we toast, Cabot?"

"Well, there's only two of us here. Why not to us?"

"Great idea. I'll drink to that. My turn. Here's to righting the wrongs of the world."

"No politics tonight, music man."

"Not before dinner anyway, Boston lady."

And after dinner."

"I have something important to tell you."

"Do tell? Want to give me a hint?"

"Not a chance. Leave 'em guessing is my motto."

They ate in silence, savoring the extraordinary smoothness and full body of the Petrus, and giddily wiping tomato sauce off their lips with expensive damask napkins. The Bolero was resonating around the room, and with each crescendo Jennifer Cabot's face became more flushed.

"The wine becomes you, Jen."

"Ravel does more. I'm feeling it all the way down, south of my navel."

DC jumped up, startling her out of the dreamy mood. He pushed the eject button and sat down on the couch. His eyes signaled that she do the same.

"In a moment, DC. I have to do the dishes. Hold your thought."

"Not tonight, hostess lady. Leave them for the cleaning lady. The thought won't hold. We have to talk now. Rather I have to talk and you have to listen."

"After all that Petrus, together with the Bolero, I'm fair game for anything. Make your pitch, DC, I'm ready to convert."

"I wouldn't think of taking advantage of someone in your condition. Remember, last night I told you that trying to convert you was out of the question."

"Then what?"

"I want to recruit you."

"Recruit me? For what? And it doesn't sound very romantic. I think I'd rather be converted."

"Forgive me, Jen, for blurting it out like that. Kinda crude and crass. What I really want...what I mean is I want you with me."

"That's the crumbiest proposal I've ever heard."

"I'll try to get better later. Right now I'm all tongue-tied. It seems my tongue got caught in my eye tooth and I can't see what I'm saying."

"I guess the wine got to you, too."

"Maybe. But I'm sober now and think I've got it all together. What I'm trying to say is that I want to recruit you for a cause that will change the political landscape of Washington, and hopefully the country."

"Oh, no, DC, I will not march in the upcoming Million Man Black Power Protest Parade."

"No marching. With those high heels you wear, you wouldn't last five blocks. Maybe less."

"Ok, no marching. No protests. What the hell do you want me for?"

"Look Jen, I know I have been bumbling along, but now it's serious time. Seriously, what I have to say is of the utmost importance. Can I count on you to keep a secret, Jennifer Cabot?"

"Of course. I grew up learning to keep secrets, even State secrets that I heard family members and important political friends discuss at private lunches and dinners. The Cabot household was a bastion of secrets. No leaks from that group. Or me."

"Okay. I believe you. Now listen with both ears and do not interrupt. I stress do not.

I'm not who you think I am. Hopping on the liberal bandwagon was the way I made my reputation, made my show the number one radio show in the Washington area. Sure, my music and the approach I took to present that music helped. However, it was the causes I championed, the money I raised, the disenfranchised I fought for and believed I was in their corner that gave me the power of celebrity. That made me King of the Hill.

That's not who Dancy Carter really is.

I'm a closet radical, slightly to the right of Genghis Khan and a disciple of his search, destroy and burn policy. Not in a violence sense, but politically.

I am part of a secret society that has opened the door for some of the most important people in Washington to pass through. Senators, CEOs, military personnel of the highest rank, scientists, actors, media executives and even a former Secretary of Defense.

A secret society that was formed to protect the rights of white America from the tentacles of blacks, blood-sucking Jews, other hybrids, immigrants that won't speak English…along with the ACLU, Planned Parenthood and NOW. Those who use every subterfuge to subvert our Constitution."

Jennifer Cabot could barely breathe. Her mouth was open trying to say something, anything, but her tongue refused to cooperate. Her eyes never left his, and widened with each statement he made. She never blinked, not wanting to miss one word, one nuance.

"They all came to the table writing a check each year for $200,000. The organization is called AFTRA, a little joke of mine since it has no connection with the union for radio and television actors.

AFTRA stands for the Association for Tyranny and Rebellion in America. I'm not the boss man of this group, but a key player.

We're not a hate group, Jen, although left-wingers might say so if they knew we existed. Right now they don't. We all are patriotic Americans dedicated to change. To make White America Right America. Dedicated to giving our country back to the hardworking people whose jobs and standards of living are threatened by illegal immigrants, self-serving trade agreements by a greedy, big business first, profit above all government that jeopardizes White American jobs by moving them overseas.

We are out to protect those whose rights are diminished daily by those who receive special privileges because of race or color.

That's it, Jen. All of it. I realize this is not a very romantic monologue, but I want to recruit you to be part of our crusade. I know you'd be perfect. I want you to be with me body and soul. I need your love, your support emotionally, fervently and yes financially. I need you to recruit your close friends and family members who think our way.

If you don't buy into AFTRA, then I need your pledge that you never reveal anything I've told you here. I trust you on this. This is a long-term project that will move slowly, deliberately, secretly, but within the law. Our members in government, the legal profession and the media are working diligently to enact changes in current legislation and changing the makeup of bureaucratic agencies to level the playing field for our kind of people.

We are not hot-headed radicals, Jen. We're practical patriots. God-fearing Americans who loathe violence. Don't condone the tactics that hate groups use. We will do it the way our forefathers did. Writing a new Constitution, establishing new rules of governing. The right way. The white way."

"DC, I am speechless. Who'd a thunk it? You the ultimate champion of the disenfranchised, disavowing all the causes you diligently worked for, to be part of a cause that seems almost impossible to make work. Yes, I've often thought that white America was getting the short end of the stick, but never believed anything could be done about it.

How long has, what is it, AFTRA, been in existence? And boy is that a brilliant acronym."

"Over two years. 26 months of blood, sweat and tears. Walking on eggs. The boss man and I recruiting, organizing, getting the bucks. Literally waiting to be exposed.

His idea was to be sure that our members were unaware of many of their fellow members. Secrecy and little connection was the plan. We met on and off with only those that were needed to implement a specific project. Specific assignments were given through encrypted e-mail. There was no timetable for completion. Slow but steady was our motto."

"My God, DC are you making all this up? Is this some kind of black humor? Or has the wine loosened your brain cells creating a disconnect with your tongue? This is like finding out that my father was a Lodge not a Cabot. All kidding aside, DC, aren't you reaching for something beyond your grasp? Hoping to pull off the deception of all time?

You can rationalize all you want about doing things legally, but to my untrained legal mind it sounds like something that could lead to big legal trouble. Jail time, I mean, for sedition or whatever. And for what? Why jeopardize a great career, a unique standing in the community; the unequivocal love of thousands of your faithful listeners; the number one radio show; a lifestyle anyone would kill for?

Let me suggest a more prudent idea. Why not just change your politics from liberal to conservative? Politicians change party affiliations and their position on the issues as easily as you change your socks. And I might add their constituents rarely penalize them for it. Radio land will believe you've had an epiphany. They'll buy it because they'll buy anything you say. That silvery tongue, unmatched intellect and downright sincerity.

I'm sure they'll believe your change of ideology is for the good. Their good. Just sell them on the idea that you're tired of hitting your head against a stone wall in battling for lost causes. That you're joining the one-time adversaries to change them."

"That sounds good if you can say it fast, Jen. No matter how I try to be convincing, hypocritical is where it will end. No matter how convincing you think I am, how do I explain my suddenly turning right after driving left for so long? The wolves will be out in force. Loyal fans will rebel. The media will crucify me.

I'll be laughed off the air.

I won't risk being humiliated. Remaining a rebel with a cause is the only way to keep my persona from being destroyed. My celebrity intact. To keep 'DC ON THE AIR' a big profit maker for WTOP and maybe keep your job in place."

"How can you live with the deception, DC? What happens when you turn right instead of left by mistake, or being confused?"

"I've thought long and hard about that, Jen. That's when I'll use my charm and word skills to explain why I walked away from championing liberal causes. Lost causes, that is, and getting behind real causes for the good of America. For white Americans."

"Sure you will, DC. That's assuming you're not indicted, labeled a racist or strung up in effigy by everyone who is not white."

"Don't look at the dark side, Jen. The light has been shining on DC since I set foot in this town and I'll keep it shining. Try and understand."

"I am, desperately. I'm trying, but I..."

"But I what? Does that mean you have reservations about us? That you like the old DC better than the new one? AFTRA would be a hollow endeavor if I thought it could turn you away from me. I need you. I want you. I want your support, not your money."

"What about love, DC? Is that something I'm to take for granted?"

"I thought you knew how I felt, Boston lady."

"Yeah, but a lady likes to hear those words. I didn't say you'd lose me. Either my support or my money. Just wanted you to be aware there was a quagmire out there. Quicksand that you will have to skirt around or sink up to your expensive silk tie."

"I understand."

"For the record, I was wild about the cool, aloof, ultra liberal Dancy Carter before you acknowledged I existed, much less knew anything about AFTRA. The new you will not make any difference in how I feel. Still wild about you. Adds a few new worry lines to my quickly aging brow though. With that out of the way, let's get down to the business of Jennifer Cabot and AFTRA. When can I join? Where do I sign? Who do I make the check out to?"

"None of the above, Jen. We're a secret society. There's no record of membership. No office for people to meet around the water cooler. No bank account. No secret handshake. You're in as of now. We'll talk about the check another time. However, there is one ritual that seals the deal. Raise your glass. Jennifer Cabot, with a sip of this marvelous ambrosia, you are officially inducted into AFTRA. Salut. Congratulations.

I must confess that this is the first time an induction was celebrated with a $250 bottle of Chateau Petrus. Drink up, lady. We can't waste a drop, right? Uh, oh, you're not smiling at my funny, Jen. You're frowning."

"Just a niggling thought just crept in. That all your expression of love is part of a game to recruit a Cabot for AFTRA. And what about the chocolate cookie?"

"Get those thoughts out of your head. My love is real and a Cabot recruit is not such a big deal with all the other important people on board. As for the chocolate cookie, she's out. Out of my apartment. Out of my life as of this afternoon. Out as in forever.

Just know that for the first time since AFTRA was created I have allowed my heart to outvote my brain; placed my overactive libido in limbo for a woman.

You, Jen. You are that woman. I've lowered my guard and made myself vulnerable to being found out. Not a pleasant prospect. My current DC life is in your hands. Jeopardizing the Dancy Carter everyone thinks they know for the Dancy Carter everyone doesn't. If that doesn't wipe away any doubt I'm in a pickle.

I love you Boston lady and trust you with the complete knowledge that I have opened a door that could reveal AFTRA to the outside world."

"No doubts, DC. You can shut that door. Your secret is safe. As for the love part, we are wasting precious minutes. Ravel's bolero is still doing strange things with parts of my body. Enough conversation. Let's make love and seal our deal with passion, not politics."

* * *

"DC back with you great folks in D.C. with 'DC ON THE AIR' on WTOP 1500 on your AM dial, where great music is the name of the game.

It's 2:22 PM and at the bottom of the hour we'll update weather and news, business news, too, with Jack and Jill Boyd.

Well I hope you're in a swinging mood after hearing that great Glenn Miller Classic 'In the Mood.' Mr. Miller was my favorite big band bandleader. Not only a wonderful musician and arranger, but for those who didn't know, a war hero as well. Captain Glenn Miller brought musical joy to thousands of G.I.'s during World War II, but died tragically when his plane crashed into the English Channel. His body was never recovered, but his great music lives on.

Captain Glenn Miller proved that music is mightier than bombs. And so if yesterday's guest, Senator Harris, is listening, I hope and pray he reappraises his position on that swollen military budget and sees fit to allocate some of those billions to fund more school construction, to help educating our kids and feed the millions living below the poverty line. Bombs don't educate or feed the needy, Senator.

Now I've said my piece and I'm glad. Call in to 800-777-DCDC if you wish to let me know how you feel. Pro or con. I'll make sure the honorable Senator gets an honest count of your comments. That's 800-777-DCDC. But you know that.

Okay, Zack, enough with politics. Let's get back on track with music. Before we go to break, 'Let's Dance' with the great Benny Goodman."

"DC!"
"Yeah, Zack."
"The boss lady is on the horn."
"How does she sound?"
"Mad as a swarm of bees without pollen."
"Hi, Jen."
"Don't hi me, Mr. Carter."
"Mr. Carter? That bad, eh?"
"Bad is an understatement. You broke your pledge to me by needling Senator Harris without giving him a chance to respond."
"He's welcome to call 800-777-DCDC. I'll open my mike to catch his comments. How about that?"
"You arrogant SOB. Are you spitefully flying in the face of the FCC regulation, just when license renewal comes up in two days?"
"Two days?"
"Don't interrupt. Are you so conflicted with your secret AFTRA that nothing else matters? Don't you care

about the station, your show, your audience, if you're taken off the air? And what about me?"

"Taken off the air? That bad, huh?"

"That bad you egomaniac. And probably out of my hands."

"Jen, please. Chew me out. Take away my mike. Shorten my coffee break...

But listen up lady exec, never, ever mention AFTRA on an open telephone line. Is that clear? Do you hear me, Jen?"

She had hung up seconds before. The dead phone meant that what he said was a dead issue. He thought about calling her back. On second thought, he thought better of it.

"Who cares about the FCC, about Jennifer Cabot trying to rein me in," he mumbled out loud. I'm DC, the number one radio man in Washington, D.C. This is my show, my audience. Nobody can tell me what to do or say. See me in court FCC if you ever try to get me off the air.

In Washington, D.C., DC is bigger than the FCC."

"Mother! It's Jennifer."

"Is that really you, daughter? So nice to hear your voice. It's been quite a while. Two weeks and 8 hours to be exact."

"I'm sorry Mother for not calling. I missed speaking to you."

"My telephone number hasn't changed, Jennifer dear."

"I know, I know. I've been very busy, Mother. My job takes up a lot of my time. Meetings, meetings."

"That's no excuse, young lady. There's an evening part of the day. Let me remind you that Grandfather Cabot was a very busy man and yet never too busy to call his favorite daughter-in-law. You have a job? HE had a government to run. Meeting with heads of State. Reading reams of classified documents late into the night. Traveling half way around the world on some diplomatic mission. No matter. He was never too busy to call."

"Yes, Mother dear. I hear you now and I heard you before when you gave me that same lecture. I know it by heart. Keep in touch, no matter what. It's a Cabot tradition. I promise, it won't happen again. I apologize."

"Accepted. So what do I owe this call today, dear girl?"

"Good news, Mother. I think I'm in love."

"You think? Now where have I heard that before?"

"Wrong choice of words. I don't think, I know. It's the real thing."

"Wonderful! Who's the unlucky boy, Jennifer? What family in Boston will be disappointed that their precious, heir-to-a fortune wastrel son is not going to become part of the Cabot family?"

"Don't be cynical, Mother. And it's not anyone in Boston. It's right here in Washington."

"Pray tell. What family in this hot-bed of political intrigue will get the bad news when you change your mind? Again."

"That's a low blow, Mother. Stop treating me like a reckless, ne'er do well, can't make up her mind, ditzy debutante."

"You did that all by your lovely self, dear."

"Well that's all behind me now. I'm a grown woman. Mature. Responsible. Not into games. Gainfully employed. Remember, I don't just have any old job. I'm an important executive at the leading radio station in town. My society hit-and-run affairs are a thing of past."

"Yes, yes, my child. It's the real thing. I'm convinced. Now who's the real boy thing."

"Man, Mother, man. A familiar voice, Mater. You hear him every day on the radio. Those golden oldies are right up your Tin Pan Alley. You love that, maybe not his politics."

"You don't mean the DC of 'DC ON THE AIR,' Dancy Carter? Do you Jennifer?"

"That's him Mother."

"Tell me it's only a one-night stand, Jennifer. Tell me that's all it is."

"Do you think so little of me, Mother?"

" To the contrary. I think a great deal about my daughter. Who she sees, who she loves, who she marries. It's the Mother Cabot in me.

But Dancy Carter? I only pray it's a one-night-stand."

"Why? Is it his politics? A Cabot can't fall for a liberal?"

"Don't lie to me Jennifer. That's not you. When did you write the check?"

"The check for what?"

"For $200,000 to be part of his secret society, AFTRA."

"You know about AFTRA?"

"Sure do. $200,000 worth and so do Gloria Grant and Grace Baldwin."

"Mrs. Grant and Mrs. Baldwin? Does he know that they never kept a secret in their entire lives? They are the Boston gossip mongers."

"The money, dear daughter. The money was more important than their keeping a secret."

"Wouldn't that jeopardize everything?"

"No. He had a trump card. He was counting on untold stories never to be told about them to keep his secrets safe."

"What stories?"

"Another time, dear. I must admit, however, that Dancy Carter is a charmer. We bought his line lock stock and barrel."

"I did too, Mother."

"Yes, my dear. It was easy with love in the picture. Easier for me. Born and bred in Charleston, I'm a red-blooded daughter of the South with a little bit of the Boston Brahmin blue blood injected by your father. The one color I have an aversion to is black. Dancy Carter talked about White America being Right America, and that sold us all instantly."

"No doubts at all?"

"I did have a niggling doubt that he was a con man, but that was dispelled when he named some of the influential people who were on board. We signed immediately."

"He gave you names? He never mentioned one to me. In fact it was made perfectly clear that no member knew about any other member. That there was never a meeting of the entire membership. Only pocket meetings with a select few were the order of business. Everything was on a need to know basis and everyone didn't need to know."

"Very clever, eh daughter? Every member thinks he's special. A big cog in a wheel that'll change America. A pretty good ploy if a con game is being played out."

"Mother, I'm stunned he never mentioned you, or Mrs. Grant or Mrs. Baldwin. Have you ever been part of a pocket meeting?"

"Never. I asked about the money allocation and all he could offer up was it being used judiciously for legislation and lobbying. My being part of a meeting was not necessary for the time being. As I see it the time being is never."

"I'm in shock, Mother. I can't believe he could bare his soul about his feelings for me, and how he trusted me with knowing about AFTRA, and not mean a single thing he said."

"Easy, my dear innocent, gullible, love-sick daughter. Lust overrode honesty and truthfulness. Money, also, has a way of bringing out the deceit in a man."

"Have we been taken in?"

"Not sure, yet. Maybe time will tell. For now I'll give him the benefit of the doubt. The idea behind AFTRA is a very attractive one for my vision of America. If leading a double life can help him pull off his vision of America, then we all profit.

Who did you make out your check to?"

"J. Bender. I thought it was odd, but he said it was for secrecy. And you, Mother?"

"A Jerome Bender, and for the same reason."

"Did yours clear?"

"Yes, some bank in the Grand Cayman Islands."

"That doesn't prove he's part of a scam, does it? It is a secret society. No office. No records. No bank account. No corporate registration."

"How convenient. Especially if he's playing us for fools. There is a bank account. A Mr. Jerome Bender in the Caymans."

"I'm not going to believe for one minute, Mother, that his expression of love for me, his trust in me, is taking me for a fool. This is Dancy Carter, the man in Washington, D.C., not some shadowy figure lurking in the back alleys of Georgetown."

"Alright, Jennifer, I'll trust your instincts. Things have changed. It's not the money or him. It's you. You're in love and I'm concerned what he can do to you. Keep your eyes open. Don't let love blind you to the celebrity of Dancy Carter.

Remember, he's not one of us. Don't mention my being part of AFTRA. Let's see if he tells you that another Cabot and friends are in the fold. Don't forget my telephone number, daughter."

"Or you mine, Mother."

"DC here. You're on the air, caller, on 'DC ON THE AIR,' on WTOP 1500 on your AM dial. What's your name?"

"Tom from Alexandria. Thanks for taking my call, Mr. Carter. But no thanks to your liberal, pinko views on our military/defense budget. We gotta stay strong so our enemies inside or outside this great country don't get any ideas we're weak. Senator Harris is right, Mr. Carter, and you're wrong. Dead wrong. Get with it. Keep America strong."

"Thanks, Tom, for those words of wisdom. If you're keeping score, listeners, that's one for the bad guys.

DC here. You're on the air caller, on 'DC ON THE AIR,' on WTOP 1500 on your AM dial. What's your name?"

"Blanche from D.C., DC."

"Hi Blanche. What do you have to say?"

"Love your voice, DC. Love your music. Love ya, period."

"Thanks Blanche. Is that it?"

"What else is there, DC?"

"How about your feelings on butter vs. bullets?"

"Oh that's easy, D.C. You're invited to dinner at my place anytime. I make the best biscuits in town and churn my own butter. No bullets though. I hate guns.:"

"Thanks again Blanche. Maybe some other time. Well folks an invitation for buttered biscuits is more palatable to me than having our tax dollars used for churning out more bombs than we need.

Did you hear Blanche, Senator?

One more call Zack, then we'll go back to the music.

"DC here. You're on the air caller, on 'DC ON THE AIR,' on WTOP 1500 on your AM dial. It's your nickel. What's your name?"

"Laura."

"Welcome to the show Laura. What's on your mind?"

"It's Mrs. Laura Harris, sir, with plenty on my mind. And I'm not too sure I'll be welcome when you hear what I have to say."

"Please, Laura, let me be the judge of that. Say your piece."

"You have maligned my husband's reputation by trivializing his point of view. In fact making fun of it."

"Who's your husband, Laura?"

"Senator David Harris."

"Oh, that husband."

"It's not a time for jokes, Mr. Carter. You virtually labeled him a warmonger. Nothing is further from the truth. This is a good man. A family first man. A peace-loving man. Not some wild-eyed hawk who wants more bombs to be dropped indiscriminately on unsuspecting civilians. No sir. He wants to allocate more money to keep America strong. He believes a strong military is a strong deterrent to any nation that believes we are weak and lacking the will to fight. He's a patriot, sir, and I can't say the same for you."

"Thanks for your call, Laura.

Folks you heard it all here without interruption. We air both sides of an issue and allow both sides to speak out. So I guess I'm not so one-sided after all.

Here's the bottom line folks. What you heard proves that the female of the species will fight with all her might to defend her mate. Good for him. Not so good for you and your tax dollars being used to fatten an already swollen defense budget.

Okay gang, politics time is over. Back to the best in music. In case you just tuned in, I'm DC, Dancy Carter with "DC ON THE AIR' on WTOP 1500 on your AM dial, where music makes every day a joyous one. But you know that.

For the next six minutes, joy is yours with two Glenn Miller classics, 'Little Brown Jug' and the wonderful 'Tuxedo Junction.' See you in a bit."

"Tough crowd, eh, DC."

"Yeah, but good stuff, Zack. Hope the boss lady is happy. Not to mention the FCC."

"Do you really care, DC?"

"Only because Miss Cabot wants me to."

"Do you really care, DC?"

"Not really."

"Hi folks. DC back with you. Oh, oh. The big clock on the wall says four minutes to three. Almost time to call it a day. We're gonna close the music hall with a Glenn Miller big hit, 'String of Pearls.'

So until tomorrow, same time 1:00 PM, same show, 'DC ON THE AIR', same station WTOP 1500 on your AM dial, this is DC, Dancy Carter signing off. Thanks for listening.

Let it go Zack…'String of Pearls'."

* * *

"Hello Phyllis. DC here. Tell Miss Cabot I'm on the phone. Sure, I'll wait.

Hi, Jen, still angry?"

"Not angry, DC, just disappointed. Your arrogance and lack of respect for my position at the station when you free wheel your opinions in the face of the FCC review."

"Jen, I'm truly sorry if it comes off that way. I don't mean to sound arrogant or disrespectful of you."

"That's hard to believe, Mr. Carter."

"I realize that, but I've had my way for so long that it's hard to swallow that three little letters can be so powerful to dictate what I can do on my own program. Forgive me. I'll try not to let it happen again."

"You've said that before, lover boy. That's another disappointment."

"What is?"

"Your lying to me. You spit in Laura Harris' eye with your flip, sexist remarks. That was a far cry from being fair. Downright foul if you ask me."

"Yeah, you're right. But I was just being me. Funning and maybe a tad obnoxious. Full of myself. Please don't read anymore into it."

"I try DC. I don't want to take away the things that make you so entertaining and big with our audience. That's what's doubling troubling to me. I can't stay angry at you very long, although I know they should place duct tape over those loose lips.

I shouldn't tell you, bad boy, but today I got bailed out of my dilemma. The FCC renewed our license. For the moment you're off the hook, DC."

"Hooray for the good guys. Great news, Jen."

"Not so fast, flip lips. It's not all great news."

"Oh, there's a catch?"

"Bureaucratically, yes. They put the station on probation. They want you reined in, or they'll come down real hard on us. Give me your word you'll do just that. Dancy are you listening? Grunt or groan."

"Listening, but trying hard not to hear, Jen. It won't be easy. My reputation with my listeners will be at stake. They want the forthright, smash-mouth liberalism I offer up. That's why they tune in, in big numbers. You can't take that away from them simply by telling them about the FCC. You know what they'll say? Damn the FCC. Government can't tell us what we want to hear or can't hear."

"I understand. We're still in business to make money, so I won't take your stick away. Just be fair. Say what you want, but be sure the other side says what they want to say. Without ridicule. That's all the FCC wants. Keep in mind, great one they'll be listening in. And so will I."

"You win, boss lady. I will try, so help me God, I will try."

"Don't invoke God in vain, you heathen. Trying is good enough."

"See you tonight, Jen?"

"After all that?"

"I never mix business with pleasure, beautiful one."

"Where?"

"My place. It's really humble. Not as opulent as yours and the wine is just a house red, but I do have another version of Ravel's Bolero."

"I don't know if I can take another night like last night, DC."

"We'll see. Be there at 7 PM and bring your toothbrush and a change of underwear. I think it's going to be a long night's journey into day."

"Mr. B., Dancy Carter."

"Great. Everything is going great. Signed up another Cabot and there could be more to come from that family and friends.

No, she doesn't know about her mother. At least I don't think so. I haven't told her. You think I should? Maybe you're right. I'll do it soon, very soon. It won't help our fragile relationship if she finds out from the matriarch herself that she's in the fold.

I don't know how she'll react, but I guess it's better to be safe than sorry. What's going on, Mr. B.? Anything I should be aware of? Some of the natives are getting restless and want to be in on what's happening. Some sort of progress report, I mean.

Oh, that's good news about Senator Harris's bill. Can I pass that on to my audience before the news actually hits the wires? Could show I have the inside track at what's happening on the Hill.

Yeah, you're right. My snapping at his heels is paying off. With that kind of support for his bill, you can be sure that many democrat sponsored social programs for blacks, education and other entitlements will be watered down. That'll evoke a lot of calls from my liberal listeners complaining that the right is winning out.

I think I'll also take on those dark-skinned bunnies at the NAACP about not doing enough to help their own people get jobs or getting out the vote. Jennifer Cabot will go nuts and have enough ammunition to book the head of the NAACP to refute what I've been saying.

What a brouhaha that will create.

The right wingers will flood the phones with protests that blacks will be asking the government to give them an edge on white America. They'll be vocal. Boy will they be vocal. And I'll have to take the brunt of their invective. But what the hell, that's what my role is being part of AFTRA. Right, Mr. B?

Right. I shouldn't forget the Jews. I'll target all those Jewish organizations for their failing to be more aggressive in combatting anti-Semitism. That they shouldn't let the hate-mongers off the hook. The hate-mongers will clog the phone lines castigating me for being a Jew-lover. I can hear it now: The Jews own the banks; they run the movie industry; Israel gets billions of our tax dollars for their security.

What about the security of the Palestinians? I'll go after those Jew haters with a vengeance. Poke fun at who they are, what they are. Cut them off. Denigrate them. That should raise the rhetoric temperature so high that Jennifer might have to bring in a PLO representative to counter my unfair characterizations.

Fairness. That's what the FCC equal time doctrine wants from DC. She'll be on my case in a minute.

Thank you, Mr. B. I appreciate your kind words and support. Although I must confess, I have to swallow my tongue every time I say a good word about all the people and things we feel are bad. Everything that AFTRA is against. Speak to you again. Give my regards to Mrs. B."

"DC back with you with a last hour surprise on 'DC ON THE AIR' on WTOP 1500 on your AM dial. And you ain't heard nothing like this from the music man before. We have scoured the entire D.C. area and found homegrown, young talent with big talent, big pipes ready to sing their little hearts out for you. D.C.'s own Chickie Files of Piano Jazz fame, and his swinging trio, will provide backup for these remarkable kids.

So unclog your ears and get ready for a live songfest. That's right, live performers doing their thing for you. And it's free—no cover charge. Remember these names folks. Marcy Mills and Barry Broom. And remember you heard them first on 'DC ON THE AIR' on WTOP 1500 on your AM dial.

Chickie, are you ready? Okay, then give me an A. That's the key, maestro. And now ladies and gentlemen, for a first on radio, the lovely Marcy Mills singing an Ella Fitzgerald classic, 'A Tisket a Tasket.' Close your eyes, people, and you'll swear it's Ella herself. Marcy Mills. Remember that name."

"DC back here folks. How about that young lady. Terrif, I say. Ella would have been proud. And Marcy is only 16 years old. What a future for her. Thank you Marcy Mills. Next up live on "DC ON THE AIR' on WTOP 1500 on your AM dial is the fabulous voice of…"

"Ladies and gentlemen, this is news director Dick Stanton. We interrupt "DC ON THE AIR' to bring you late breaking news, tragic news of a fire bombing of the Planned Parenthood Clinic in downtown Washington. The bomb went off about 2:08 PM. Details are sketchy at this time, but we do know that three women were injured, one seriously. All were taken to the George Washington Medical Center. At this time the police report no clues as to who might be responsible for the bombing , and no one has claimed to be involved. However, they are searching for a gray BMW sedan spotted racing away from the scene as the bomb exploded. More details later on the 2:30 news break with Jack and Jill Boyd. We now return to 'DC ON THE AIR' with your host Dancy Carter."

"That's terrible news, Dick. What maniac is out there blowing up a clinic and injuring innocent people for some misguided cause? If anybody in my listening area has information about that gray BMW or about who may have perpetrated this dastardly crime, call 911 or DC here at 800-777-DCDC. We'll keep your tip anonymous. My prayers are with the injured women.

I realize that this egregious crime makes it difficult to get back to our program, but life goes on. And so does 'DC ON THE AIR.' Chickie, tickle those 88's and let us welcome our next young future star, Barry Broom. Barry is only 15 years old, and a budding Billy Eckstine sound-alike. Barry will be giving us his rendition of that great Billy oldie, 'I Apologize.'

"Barry Broom, folks. Remember that name."

"Jen, welcome to my less than humble abode."

"Modesty is not your strong suit, music man. This is a neat looking place. Very masculine and good taste. Love that Frank Stella over the leather sofa, too. Where do I put my toothbrush?"

"Right next to my Water PIK in the master bathroom. I call it the master bathroom but it is really the mister bathroom, there is no other bathroom."

"Makes sense. If an egomaniac has any sense.

That was terrible news about that explosion at the clinic. Dick Stanton's face was ashen white when I saw him in the news room. His daughter works at the clinic."

"Is she okay?"

"Yes, she was out of the office at the time."

I hate to ask, DC, but was that an AFTRA target?"

"No way. I told you we are non-violent. That is not how we operate. Besides, it messed up my live program."

"It messed up some women's lives, too, don't you think?"

"Sorry, I wasn't thinking clearly when I said that."

"In truth it didn't mess up your program at all. The call-in response to those kids was sensational. They could really sing. Where did you get that talent?"

"Zack did it. Scoured a number of high schools and made the recommendations as well as the idea for a live song fest. He has a great ear for talent. Does a great job as my producer/ engineer as well. I promised him a raise and he deserves one. See what you can do to do it. Soon. I would appreciate it."

"We're in sort of a wage freeze, but I'll look into it. For you."

"If it happens, boss lady, be sure you tell him it was for him."

"I don't know how you do it with a straight face, DC, but you certainly had big brass ones putting a verbal hurt on the pro-lifers who bombed that clinic. Especially since AFTRA is pro-life numero uno. How do you manage the art of deception so easily?"

"Easy in this case. Violence is not our game plan. I, we, abhor it. Remember I told you I am comfortable with my two lives. My listeners want to hear me go after the bad guys, and I give them what they want. The other side of my life is down the road. And I'll take that turn when I reach it."

"That may be too late, DC."

"Could be, but if you think I had big brass ones over that, then you're going to think I have humongous ones when I divulge a secret that might blow your mind. Just promise you won't scream or fault me for not telling you sooner." Dancy took a big breath and said, "Take a big breath and hold it. Your mother is an active dues-paying member of AFTRA."

"I knew that."

"You did?"

"Just found out, Mr. Large Brass, and I was sure you'd prove her wrong by telling me sooner rather than later."

"What does that mean?"

"She was certain you only showed interest in me because you had lust in your heart. Playing the love game was the way to satisfy that lust. And when you got my body, 'you would get my check' is the way she put it.

What she didn't know was that I was after your body and could only hope and pray that you wanted mine. Love could come later. The check was a mere pittance to pay for that to happen."

With her eyes wide open she said, "Does that sound convoluted?"

"Just a bit, but that also means she doesn't trust me. That's very troubling, as well."

"Don't let it, DC."

"Did she also tell you about Mrs. Grant and Mrs. Baldwin putting their checks in our exchequer?"

"I couldn't believe that. You might have shot yourself in the bank account with those two. They are Boston's biggest blabbermouths. Gossip is their stock in trade. They could put your secret, private society in public jeopardy. Mother hinted that you had something on them. Like what?"

"They know that I know about their wild parties with Harvard underclassmen when their husbands are out of town."

"You resorted to blackmail? How low could you get?"

"Not low at all. Just a hint of persuasion to keep their lips sealed."

"How did you dredge up that juicy information?"

"Mama Cabot dredged it up for me."

"I can't believe my prim and proper society mother would dish out dirt on her two best friends."

"She may have lacked faith in me, but dear mama had great faith in AFTRA. This is the kind of right wing operation she believes in, and wants to succeed."

"Risky, DC. Very risky."

"Not much. One phone call to the gossip twins and they made the Sphinx seem like a chatterbox."

"If I've learned anything about you, DC, it is never to underestimate your ability to play the female of the species like a drum. Yours truly included."

"Flattery will get you somewhere...if you play your cards right, Boston lady."

"I'm counting on that, music man."

"Bet on it. Meanwhile pour the wine while I get into my seducing-producing smoking jacket, sans the pipe. Dinner will be here shortly from Dukes. Hope you like what I ordered."

"I love a crab meat cocktail and rare Prime Rib. That's exactly what my taste buds are primed for."

"How did you make such a lucky guess?"

"No matter that you charm the hell out of us females, you are very predictable. No guess, Mr. Carter. I never forget to remember the meal that seduced me the first time."

"You got me there. Put Ravel's Bolero on and make yourself comfortable on the couch. See what that does to your seduction level."

"Forget the couch. Take me to your master bedroom, master."

"Who'll answer the door when the food arrives?"

"Pin a note out there for the delivery boy to leave it, and leave a big tip."

"Poses a little problem, lady executive. The icy cold crab meat will get warm and the hot Prime Rib will get cold."

Unbuttoning her blouse, Jennifer said, "I couldn't care less, just as long as we heat up your bed. Let's get it on now and eat later."

DC rolled his eyes and quipped, "And they said the Boston Cabots were cold, dispassionate people. I'll never believe that rumor again."

"Mr. B., Dancy Carter. I know, I know damn well I'm not to call you at the office unless it's an extreme emergency. Well it's urgent for me. I'm really pissed off, not to mention disturbed about that bombing. How could you sanction a violent act like that at the clinic? Picketing, protesting that's okay, but bombs are not what AFTRA is all about. We're non-violent. Right? We do things within the law. Right? No one would ever get hurt. Right? Well sir, the use of a fire bomb is not a legal act, and people did get hurt.

It's all most troubling to me, and I question if I want to be part of a group that advocates terror and violence. AFTRA is at risk and yours truly is at risk if anyone starts sniffing around. They might pick up our scent. If it happens to be my scent, I'm through in radio, in Washington, and certainly lose any effectiveness as a point man for you. No more 'DC ON THE AIR' would be the price I pay. Maybe even jail time. Not good for you, and painstakingly bad for me."

Yes, sir. I've said my piece. Go ahead, but it better be more than it won't happen again.

Say that again? AFTRA was not involved. An anonymous call to the police from a radical pro-life group claiming responsibility? Oh, god. That's great news, and I'm sorry for running off at the mouth. I should have known better. What can I do to wipe the egg off my face?

Great idea. I'll tell my listeners that this group involved should be prosecuted to the fullest extent of the law. Right. I'll ask them to call in and voice their indignation for such a violent act, regardless of their position on choice.

"Yeah, that's good too. Visit the injured lady in the hospital. I'll bring her flowers and some good old fashioned DC cheering up. And play her favorite song on my next show. Thanks for that. You know, this may be a blessing in disguise. Some callers may feel that my pro-choice stance gives those who condone abortion the right to keep murdering defenseless children. I'm responsible for the bombing in a strange way. The right-to-life people will agree. The pro-choice do-gooders will say I made the right choice in advocating choice.

We win both ways.

I'm sorry, Mr. B., for mouthing off before I knew what you knew. I promise not to be so judgmental, thinking that AFTRA could ever be involved in a violent act.

Regards to Mrs. B."

"Good morning sir, I'd like to talk to Zack Zolo."

"Sorry, you have the wrong number."

"Zack? You are Zack Zolo. I'd know that voice anywhere. This is Brian Dobbs."

"Yeah, I know who this is, but Zack Zolo doesn't exist anymore. My name is Zack Zoltowsky and I have nothing to say to anyone from the FBI."

"Zolo, Zoltowsky, who cares? This is Dobbsie. Your partner at the bureau for ten years. Your friend for longer."

"What do you want Brian?"

"Hey, I know you're bitter because the bureau ran you off the reservation for being drunk on a stakeout."

"Allegedly drunk. What do you want, Mr. Dobbs?"

"Did I say I wanted anything? Can't a friend call an old friend? Just wanted to say hello and find out how my old partner is doing these days."

"Former partner. The friend part is highly suspect. Where was my friend when I was being railroaded?"

"May I explain?"

"Don 't really care. Anything to do with you, any agent or the bureau itself is stored away for good in my attic. Now let's get real, Dobbs. What's the reason for the call? The bureau doesn't call to say hello and renew old friendships to someone they consider a pariah."

"Believe me, Zack, I tried every which way to Sunday to support you. They made it clear it was you or my career. I was a coward and took the easy way out. Or it seemed easy back then. I had to keep my badge and protect my pension. I regret that decision every day and apologize for not explaining my position. The Director left me no options. Steer clear of Zack Zolo or face dismissal. I was in a bind. My family or friendship."

"Doesn't fly, Dobbs. You could have called me on the sly, if nothing else, to offer support. You didn't then and now you're a closed book with me. For the record, though, I come from the old school where friends don't ignore friends. No matter what. In any case that was an eternity ago and apologies won't cut it. Now let's cut the crap, ditch the apology and tell me the real reason for the call."

"You were a great agent, Zack. The senior guy who taught a junior one everything. The Bureau made a huge mistake, a grievous mistake and lost a valuable agent. But that's irrelevant. You may have had to turn in your badge, but you can't turn away from years of service to your country."

"I have no idea where you're going, Dobbs, but the stuff is starting to pile up. Give up the real reason for the call or this conversation is over. Got it?"

"It's classified Zack, but I'll make an exception for an agent who had clearance at one time."

"Between us 'agents' everything the bureau does is classified. So now one more time, why the call?"

"We have info that a subversive group is operating right here in the nation's capitol. They have grandiose plans of rewriting the Constitution and taking over the country."

"What else is new, Dobbs? There must be dozens of groups like that you're tracking all the time. What's so unusual about this group?"

"They're different. As far as we can determine this is not some small-time group working out of a loft in a vacant building, with a cell phone for a telephone system. This is a star-studded group of VIPs from all walks of the political spectrum and more. All very smart, politically connected, and to the right of Attila the Hun. They have money to burn and operate secretly."

"Good bureau work, Brian. Do you think that for one moment they would operate openly? And why not shut them down if they really exist?"

"I believe they exist. Call it agent instinct. Just can't pin anything down."

"Seeing ghosts again, Dobbs? That's what you did years ago."

"A little more this time. I got an anonymous tip from someone who said he was recruited. Admittedly what he said was sketchy and uncorroborated. Nothing in any of our files."

"Did he name names?"

"Not exactly. Said there were Congressmen, Military, CEOs and media personalities who have already infiltrated many of our institutions and Congressional committees."

"Isn't that enough to work on?"

"Can't get a handle on it yet."

"Did he name his recruiter?"

"Only that it was a Mr. B."

"Did you ever think he was some kind of conspiracy kook that was cooking up a story to get you chasing your tail?"

"Yeah, but it sounded real enough."

"In your head, Dobbs. You fell for that same kind of stuff years ago. Uncorroborated. No names. No nothing. This is a secret society, so secret it sounds like a conspiracy concocted by a paranoid, reincarnated J. Edgar Hoover. A pure fantasy."

"You may be right, but when I brought it to the Director's attention, he said go with it. It is our duty to investigate something like this until we find out it's nothing. We protect the Constitution, partner, and we treat rumor, innuendo and uncorroborated tips as if they were real things."

"Yeah, I know how it used to work, but I couldn't care less now. Even if I did care, I have nothing to offer. I'm in the private sector and government work—FBI particularly—doesn't appeal to me."

"Well partner, I know you care, and in fact can help. You're a big-time radio producer working with a well-known radio personality in D.C. Possibly you've heard something, anything that can help me zero in on this group. Assuming it exists."

"Cut the partner stuff, Dobbs. And are you suggesting that Dancy Carter is somehow involved?"

"No, no, not at all. I was referring to your job as a producer."

"Dobbs, your information about me is as flawed as your uncorroborated, no names, anonymous informants' tips. I am only a small-time engineer on a local radio station with the meaningless title of producer. Nothing big-time at all. It just sounds good on my resume and entitles me to an additional $100 a week, by union pay scale guidelines."

"Oh, come now, Zack. Just like the old days, you still underestimate your smarts, your instincts, those impeccable investigative skills. That self-effacing, self-deprecating persona may give those who don't know you the impression that you're slow-witted, just this side of incompetent, but not to me partner. I know the real Zack Zolo. He's top drawer."

"For the last time, Dobbs, we're not partners. And it's Zoltowsky. Blow smoke in another direction. Hear me?"

"Whatever! Zolo, Zoltowsky, you were the best of the best. And there's a great deal you can do. You know D.C. and meet all the VIPs who appear on Carter's show. You talk to all kinds of people when you screen calls for the call-in segments. There are things you can pick up."

"You seem to know an awful lot about how the show works, don't you, Dobbs? Didn't know our signal got as far as Boston."

"That's my job, Zack. I mentioned all of this to the Director and he's impressed. I told him if anyone can pin down info on whether or not this group exists, you are the guy. The past is past, and he authorized me to offer you a temporary assignment with the Bureau at your old grade level. That's good money, Zack, and should help put that son of yours through one of D.C.'s top colleges."

"Are you taking something in the arm, Dobbs? You want me to go to work for the bureau that tried to destroy me? A job that was so abhorrent to me that I've buried it deep in the recesses of my mind, as if it never existed. And vowed never to retrieve it. Now I have an uncomplicated job. No intrigue in life. All I do is spin records and revel in being part of 'DC ON THE AIR,' the most popular show in Washington, D.C. No bad guys shooting at me. The only weapon I carry is my cell phone. The only badge I wear is the ID that gets me past security at the front desk. The only buttons I push increase the volume gain when it's commercial time.

So Mr. Dobbs, with all due respect to our non-existent friendship, my answer is thanks, but no thanks. If that's too difficult to understand, then how about NO in capital letters. Even if I had anything to offer, I don't want to help you or the Bureau."

"I understand clearly, Zack, but please think it over. Sleep on it. I don't blame you for feeling this way, because I didn't help you in your hour of need back when. It's different now, since I went way out on a limb with the Director, because I know you can help. This is not easy for me to eat crow. And I realize that I never can make up for what I did to our partnership, much less our friendship. I can only appeal to your patriotism. If this secret group does exist then you would be doing yeoman service for your country."

"Sure, Dobbs. You said that with a straight face. I can see the flag waving in the breeze. However, let's not be naïve. We both know that your offer is the Bureau's way of salving their conscience for what they did. Right?"

"Probably."

"Probably, my eye. That's what the Bureau does best. Try to make a bad decision a good one without ever admitting the bad decision in the first place. I've said enough and heard more than enough, Dobbs. My hearing mechanism has reached the maximum fatigue stage. We're through. Don't call me, I'll call you. Don't wait by the phone."

"No matter, Zack, thanks for hearing me out. It was nice talking to my old partner again."

"I wish I could say the same, Dobbs."

When Zack hung up, he was totally washed out. His shirt soaked through and through with perspiration. He grabbed a beer out of the fridge and sat down in his favorite lounge chair. He tried desperately to get Brian Dobbs out of his mind. It was difficult. His mind was racing a mile a minute and kept repeating DOBBS, DOBBS, DOBBS.

The hair was standing up on the back of his neck as he tried to fathom why Dobbs would appear out of the blue and with such a weird, unconvincing story. There had to be more. But what? The Bureau doesn't divulge anything to anyone if it's classified. Especially to a "civilian," unless they have an ulterior motive. Brian Dobbs was one of the smartest agents he knew. An agent who believed in the Bureau right or wrong. It wasn't protocol for an agent to go directly to the Director. Channels the first order of business to get clearance. And clearance for a disgraced, one-time agent an absolute no no. The FBI gets hundreds of tips, most anonymous, every day like the one Dobbs outlined. What was it in this one that made the Director break house rules and try to bring Zack Zoltowsky on board? Or did Dobbs make up the Director story and was on his own?

This was a puzzlement. Yet maybe a clue was the part that Dobbs sort of threw away. That a radio personality was part of that secret group. Although he denied it, was he alluding to Dancy Carter?

It had to be, or else why would he stoke up the cold ashes of a long burnt-out friendship. Much less dangle the carrot of money, his old grade level, and openly admit what he didn't do, or that the Bureau had made a terrible mistake.

It had to be they knew more than Dobbs was alluding to. Smart agents are like smart lawyers. They never ask a question that they don't know what the answer will be. Or part of the answer. There's a piece of the puzzle that Dobbs wants to fit into the picture. And wants Zack Zoltowsky to furnish it.

What piece?

Dancy Carter? Is he the piece? Dobbs knows more than he's letting on about DC and wants the "Producer" to make the puzzle whole. Zack felt that this was illogical logic. That the FBI, Dobbs specifically, didn't know Dancy Carter like he did. Sure he's been a little loose with ethnic smears, but he was just funning. Pulling my leg, as he put it. Maybe so. Probably so, because the real Dancy Carter is into every liberal cause on the planet. Not a right wing bone in his body.

Dobbs should listen to him cross swords with a Senator who wants to increase defense spending and votes to cut education spending. Or Congressmen who would love to see <u>Roe v. Wade</u> repealed. Racists who believe that blacks have an unfair advantage over whites. Jew haters who believe every administration gives far too much aid to Israel and virtually ignores the plight of the Palestinians.

It's possible that some media VIP could be involved, assuming that secret right wing group really exists, but it can't be the Dancy Carter he works with. The DC that is lionized by the ACLU, the Anti-Defamation League, the NAACP and NOW without them finding him out. Somehow, someway they would sniff it out.

That's logical, not illogical.

"No, Mr. Dobbs," he yelled out loud, "show me the beef and maybe, just maybe I'll help. Until then let me be."

As Zack started to get out of the chair, he realized that his left eye was twitching. In the past, when that happened, it meant his subconscious was sending him a coded message. It wasn't always easy to decode. In his agent life he could. He would look for a trigger word or thing, follow his gut instinct, and there it was. A decoding happened. This strange phenomenon happened only once since he left, or rather was unceremoniously booted out of the Bureau. That was when Carter uttered the "N" word about Billie Holiday. He couldn't believe his ears. Was it just a slip of the tongue? An aberration? Or just pulling legs. Funning. The twitching eye raised doubts about all of it. It was sending a coded message. At the time it wasn't decoded.

He now questioned whether that incident had any correlation to what Dobbs was saying; that a radio personality was part of a right wing secret group. Dancy Carter? Coincidence? Reality? The twitching eye never failed. Blurting out bigot decoded the message. Now his head was really spinning. His mind racing at two hundred miles per hour. Dancy Carter was a friend and his boss. His livelihood depended on "DC ON THE AIR' staying on the air. Yet as much as he detested the Bureau and questioned the loyalty of his former partner and friend, he knew deep down that Brian Dobbs would never concoct a scenario about a right wing secret society with a high profile membership. He knew as a former agent that gut instinct played a significant role in evaluating an informant's tip.

If someone like Dancy Carter was on Dobbs' radar screen, who better to contact than the one person who worked with that person every day. A former agent no less. Someone who understood how the game was played.

After taking a long swig of beer, he decided to keep his eyes open and his ear to the ground to anything Dancy Carter did or said that might connect the dots. Might lead to a secret group. He laughed out loud when he made that decision. It struck him that you can take the agent out of the Bureau, but you can't take the Bureau out of the agent. No matter what. He was hooked. Dobbs had stirred up something inside that he considered dead.

"Damn that misguided loyalty."

He took a final swig of beer and took the steps up to the attic.

"Good evening. Is this the residence of Mr. Dancy Carter, the radio man of 'DC ON THE AIR'?"

"One and the same. Who is this?"

"Professor Bartholomew Doyle of the Political Science Department at Boston College."

"Did my cousin flunk your course? Sorry Professor. I was just funning. What can I do for you?"

"Answer this question, sir. If any despotic regime in the Middle East believes that the increased military defense budget now being debated in Congress is defeated, due to dissenters like yourself, would that weaken the capabilities of our armed forces? Absolutely stretching them so thin that they would be ineffective? And if these regimes believe that Congress and the American people lack the will to engage in unpopular wars, will that encourage them, embolden them to stir up trouble in the region, specifically against Israel?"

"That's not a question, Professor Doyle. That's a speech you should make at the UN or before a

Congressional committee. In any case, you've caught me at the wrong time and the wrong place, sir. I don't take call-ins off the air. This is my private time. I suggest you call WTOP, after 2:00 P.M. tomorrow, and I'll be happy to discuss the subject with an open mike. Now I don't mean to be rude, Professor Doyle, but I have to hang up now."

"One more thing, Mr. Carter. I was told to call by your friend Grace Baldwin and ask about a secret right wing group that was formed to protect white American rights. Do you know about its existence?"

"Sorry, sir, I don't know a Grace Baldwin and have no idea what you are talking about. Good evening."

Dancy Carter slammed down the phone and yelled out loud. "Son-of-a-bitch. If that gossip-monger Baldwin told this guy anything about AFTRA, my world could crumble in the blink of an eyelash. Better check it out in the morning. Better still, I'll call Jennifer right now."

"Jen, am I glad you're home tonight."

"Why, lover boy? Are you looking for some action? Or checking up on me?"

"No funning lady, we have a serious problem. I just received a very disturbing call from a Political Science Professor at Boston College."

"Disturbing? How so?"

"First he asked a long convoluted question about the debate on the defense budget and how my objection to any increase might affect the voting outcome. Or worse yet, how it might affect the politics of the Middle East."

"Why disturbing? Maybe he couldn't wait to call in tomorrow and wanted to debate the subject immediately. People's passions run high when you take sides in an important issue like this, and your influence on your listeners infuriates some people. They want to be part of the debate without waiting for the proper time."

"That was my thought, until he said that Grace Baldwin suggested he ask me about AFTRA. How can that Boston blabbermouth be so stupid or careless to mention AFTRA to an outsider? Unless she's a close friend, intimate I mean, and wants to stay on the Professor's good side of the bed."

"Did he say AFTRA?"

"No, not exactly."

"What did he say?"

"That there was a secret right wing group that exists to protect White American rights. He didn't have to say AFTRA. His question made it clear that such a group actually did exist. Goddamn that Baldwin."

"I can't believe Grace would do such a thing, DC. Reneging on her promise to my mother never to reveal a thing about the group would be death to their relationship."

"Well I guess that wasn't important to keeping on the good side of a lover. In any case there's going to be hell to pay for what she did."

"Is that some kind of physical threat?"

"We'll see. Right now I need to get as much information about the Professor to determine what he really knows. Call your mother and find out what Baldwin told Doyle. And why. When I know the truth, then I will determine what to do with Mrs. Blabbermouth."

"It all has to be some kind of joke, DC. Grace Baldwin had to be her usual playful self. Just kidding around."

"This is no laughing matter, Jen. Even if she was just kidding around, it means we can't trust her. She can blab anything at any time and get the wrong people thinking the wrong way.

She can bring us down.

If this Doyle guy believes her, and acts on it, we'll have to do something about him, too."

"That sounds ominous. Is that another physical threat?"

"Let's not waste time discussing this now. Call your mother and get back to me ASAP."

Carter hung up the phone, turned off the music, poured another glass of wine and paced the floor nervously. He sensed trouble was only a phone call away.

When the telephone rang about a half hour later, he answered before the first ring had barely rung.

"DC? What took you so long to answer?"

"No time for funning, Boston lady. What did you learn?"

"Nothing!"

"Nothing?"

"Nothing that makes any sense. Grace Baldwin never heard of a Professor Bartholomew Doyle much less mentioning AFTRA to anyone. She swore to mother. Lying to her would be out of the question. Mother contacted her Provost friend at B.C. and there is no Professor Doyle on staff."

"That's even more troublesome. Doyle had my unlisted home number. Knew about AFTRA. Knew enough of my show to use that defense budget issue as a subterfuge for the real issue. My possible involvement in AFTRA. If Doyle has the info, others do too. Something is fishy, and someone is lying."

"DC, I believe Mrs. Baldwin is telling the truth. She may be a flake, and a blabbermouth, but she would never lie to mother. Mother for sure is not lying."

"Who then? Doyle didn't pull this info out of the air. More important why? Who is this Doyle character, if not a professor?"

"I'm frightened, DC. For you. For me. For Mother. And most of all for AFTRA being exposed."

"I'm with you. Let's not panic yet. Call your Mother back and ask her to use Cabot political contacts in Boston to find out if a Bartholomew, Barton or Bart Doyle works for any government agency with headquarters in the Boston area. The FBI, CIA, NSI, and House Intelligence committee or others. I will do the same in Washington. I don't want to go off half-cocked about this yet, Jen. There may be an avenue we've not considered."

"Like what?"

"An investigative reporter sniffing out a rumor he heard in a bar. Or a gung-ho Assistant D.A. looking to score points. A local cop or FBI agent acting on an informant's tip."

"That makes more sense to me, DC. But that's a pretty wide range of things to cover. Easy to panic over."

"Let's not do that. Whoever Doyle really is we can't allow him to rattle our cages. We must stay calm."

"Easy for you to say. I'm getting more jittery by the minute."

"Stay focused, Boston lady, and tell Mama Cabot to stay calm, too. Everything she does has to be matter-of-fact. No apparent urgency."

"Mother always stays calm. It's her friends that concern me."

"Right. Tell her to make sure Grace Baldwin speaks to no one. No one about anything."

"Hear you. What's next?"

"That's it. It's getting late. We'll speak in the morning. Meanwhile sleep tight tonight."

"Sleep? Are you kidding me, DC. It'll take a couple of sleeping pills to sleep tonight."

"I said sleep, not be zonked out. A nice glass of wine is a better idea. If that doesn't work, try counting sheep."

"That's an old bromide, Dancy."

"Maybe so, but when you reach 10,000 you'll be exhausted."

* * *

"Hello, D.C., and a good, good afternoon to you all. In case you haven't looked at your watch, it's 1:00 PM. Time for 'DC ON THE AIR' on WTOP 1500 on your AM dial. I'm DC, Dancy Carter along with Mr. Zack, my favorite producer. We're ready, willing and able to bring you some exciting music from way back when, and maybe a hot topic or two for discussion on our call-in around 2 PM. Great music, great discussion. Ah, but you know that.

First, a little weather update for any of my shut-in friends in DC land. It's cool and crisp with temperature at 50 degrees. Probably going down a few degrees by the time DC leaves the air. No matter what's happening outside, right here I can guarantee that the music you hear will warm the cockles of your heart.

Oh yeah, one more thing. I want to report about the exceptionally successful fund raiser the other night for the United Negro College Fund. We raised a lot of the green stuff to allow many underprivileged African-American young men and women to receive the education opportunity of a lifetime: a four year scholarship to college.

The turnout was the sold out kind. VIP's everywhere. The wizard of the basketball court, Michael Jordan, the featured speaker. I thank everyone for their support. And that includes all my favorite people out there in DC land for your outpouring of pledges and checks.

Now on to DC's musical tribute on WTOP 1500 on your AM dial. A tribute to those African-American music pioneers who at the beginning of the 20th century gave birth to the blues, and created the true America music genre called Jazz. Gut-bucket New Orleans Dixieland, the soulful sounds of the Kansas City Blues, the Jumping Jazz, Chicago style.

That means Satchmo, Kid Ory, King Oliver, Jelly Roll Morton and the first diva of the blues, Bessie Smith.

First up, Louis Armstrong and the Hot Five with 'Struttin' With Some Barbecue': Satchmo on trumpet, Johnny St. Cyr on guitar, Johnny Dodds on clarinet, and the legendary Kid Ory on trombone.

"Roll it Mr. Zack."

"Great intro DC. Boy, those guys could really play."

"And how. As Satchmo would say, 'those cats can really swing.'"

"This is a two minute break, DC. Want some coffee?"

"No thanks. This foot-stomping stuff has me wired enough without adding caffeine to the mix."

"Sorry I missed the fund raiser. An old buddy dropped in unexpectedly and we talked for hours. I forgot the time. Brian Dobbs and I go back a long way. Families, too. He's the Director of Field Operations for the FBI in Boston. I did send a check, though."

"Boston? That's Cabot territory. Does he know the boss lady?"

"I have no idea."

"Well, in any case, we missed you my friend. Even Michael Jordan said he missed the guy behind the controls of 'DC ON THE AIR' who roots for his Washington Wizards. Sends his regards."

"MJ said that, DC?"

"Not just to me, Zack, but to the entire audience. You got your fifteen minutes of fame."

"Love that fame. Thirty seconds to air, DC."

"When we get back on the air for the call-in segment, if a Professor Bartholomew Doyle calls put him on hold. Don't want to talk with him."

"Personal, DC?"

"You might say that."

"You're on."

"Hi folks. This is DC back with 'DC ON THE AIR' on WTOP 1500 on your AM dial. How do you like those Jazz greats up to now? And how about that Bessie Smith? That's a lady with soul.

Ok, a change of pace. Is your finger ready to punch up our telephone number? It's call-in time. 800-777-DCDC. You have questions, DC has answers. You have comments, DC has rebuttals. It's your time on call-in time.

Open the lines, Zack.

Hi caller. This is DC. Who's this?"

"Professor Bartholomew Doyle is my name and political science is my game."

"Where do you profess at professor?"

"You know that answer Mr. Carter, since we spoke recently."

"Oh that professor. What's on your mind, sir?"

"Have you given any thought to that rumor I asked you about a secret society operating in Washington to make White America Right America?"

"I don't speculate on rumors. Zack put through the next caller.

"Hi DC here. You're on the air caller. What's your name?"

"Professor Doyle again, Mr. Carter. If you don't speculate on rumors, suppose I tell you this secret society is real."

"Don't have a clue. Thanks for calling.

Shut the phones down, Zack. Seems like there aren't any callers with issues. Real issues to discuss today.

"Hi folks, DC back on 'DC ON THE AIR' on WTOP 1500 on your AM dial. Back with a lot more of that New Orleans Jazz with the artists that nobody takes issue with.

It's a threesome. First Louis Armstrong with his famous rendition of 'Basin Street Blues,' followed by King Oliver, the legendary cornetist, with his infectious 'Dippermouth Blues.' And we'll close with the inimitable Jelly Roll Morton with his 'Doctor Jazz-Stomp.'

So that's it for DC, Dancy Carter, today. Thanks for listening. Tune in tomorrow at the same time 1:00 PM, same place WTOP 1500 on your AM dial, same 'DC ON THE AIR,' but you know that. See you Mrs. B.

Take us out Mr. Producer."

"Mr. Zoltowski, I thought I made it perfectly clear to keep that professor character on hold and not let him through. Did you hear me right?"

"He gave me a different name, DC. Didn't know it was him."

"So how did that clown get back to call again?"

"Must have had two lines open at the same time. Gave me a different name again."

"That's no excuse. You're getting paid to screen callers carefully, Mr. Engineer. Don't tell me you couldn't recognize that it was the same voice as the first one."

"I goofed, DC. I wasn't listening with both ears. It won't happen again."

"Better believe it won't happen again. Or else."

"I promise, DC."

"I can't allow some kook to waste my time and my listeners' patience with drivel. There are legitimate callers out there with legitimate issues."

"I know, I know."

"Besides, it's not good for the show's ratings to shorten the call-in segment because somebody wants to bait me with speculation. Screen Zack. Screen, goddammit. Got it?"

"Yes sir, sir."

"Zack? It's Brian."

"Wow, Brian you got Dancy's dander up. He was steaming and read me the riot act. Thought my job was gone."

"I bet. What's your take? Is Carter hiding something? Cutting me off so abruptly sounds like he is."

"I don't know what to think. DC doesn't like surprises. Rarely gives air time to a caller with a rumor."

"My kind of rumor must have touched a nerve."

"Don't think so, Brian. He debates issues no matter the ideology or the caller. He ignores rumors."

"Is he hiding something, anything?"

"I have no idea if he's hiding anything, but I think you're shooting blanks on this one."

"My gut tells me otherwise."

"No matter, Brian. I can't do what I did with you again. He reamed my ass."

"Isn't that overreacting on his part, Zack?"

"No. It's in character for him. So Mr. FBI you'd better come up with a better game plan without me, 'cause I'll be in a shitload of trouble if he ever finds out that Brian Dobbs and Professor Doyle are one and the same."

"Aren't you overreacting now?"

"No. In fact there's double trouble, since the boss lady of the station, Jennifer Cabot, was on my case more than Carter. She wasn't happy that the popular call-in segment was cut short. Ratings you know. 'DC ON THE AIR' makes big bucks with big ratings."

"Is that Jennifer Cabot of the Boston Cabots?"

"That's our boss lady."

"I know her. We met at the Cabot home in Boston at a party. They are as white right as you can get, politically. Mother Cabot wears the Confederate flag to bed."

"That's her right, Dobbs."

"Anything romantically between Carter and your boss lady?"

"If there is they keep pretty secret about it."

"You mean like that secret society, Zack?"

"That's a stretch. She may be a liberated lady, but her politics are strictly conservative. Carter is the ultimate liberal. They argue all the time about those differences when it comes to the show. The only society she's involved with is the elite 400 of Boston."

"Hard to believe that two attractive people are not attracted to each other. Instinct tells me they're getting it on."

"I have to agree, despite what I've said. My gut tells me maybe."

"Finally a ray of sanity, Zack. Once an agent always an agent. Now will you consider working with us, with me, to get to the bottom of this?"

"Stow that agent stuff, and don't get your hopes too high, Dobbs. I'll do as little as I can, but I will not jeopardize my job for your wild theory."

"Fair enough."

"And if that sounds like words spoken in the past by an agent who said he 'can't do, because family, career and pension were threatened,' you're hearing an instant replay."

"You got me on that one, Zolo."

"Zoltowski in this town. Zoltowski."

"God, this Beef Bourguignon is fantastic, Jen. I didn't know you could boil water, much less cook gourmet style."

"There's lots you don't know about me, Mr. Carter."

"Evidently. I guess all those political questions I asked at our first dinner kept me from finding out about the domestic you."

"You got that right, Mr. Washington. Cabots are social animals, and as part of my privileged life cooking was high up my education regimen. I spent many a summer vacation at L'Ecole Provence Cooking School."

"They taught you well."

"Oui, and wait till you taste my soufflé."

"Soufflé notwithstanding, Jen, do you know a Brian Dobbs?"

"The name sounds familiar. Should I?"

"You tell me."

"Well, if this is a quiz, I think a Dobbs was at one of Mother's soirees sometime ago. I believe he's the director of something in Boston. FBI, I think."

"Are you certain of that, Jen?"

"Well...FBI? My God, DC, do you think that it's a coincidence that he might be the link between Professor Doyle's calls? Or is he Dobbs posing as Doyle?"

"You tell me, Julia Childs."

"What are you inferring? That I'm the one feeding the FBI information about AFTRA, because I met Dobbs before? I can't even remember what he looked like."

"I wouldn't think that for a minute. You aren't the leak, are you Jen?"

"That question is insulting, so cut out the fooling."

"Yeah, just fooling, Boston lady."

"Thank you. However, if Doyle/Dobbs is one and the same, I'm sure you'll get to the bottom of it."

"I think I may have already."

"Are you still fooling?"

"Dead serious. I have no absolute proof, but I suspect I've found a weak link in the long chain of coincidences."

"Like what?"

"Zack Zoltowski's long time friend is Brian Dobbs."

"Friend?"

"FBI friend."

COINCIDENCE NUMBER ONE: Zack missed my fundraiser because unexpectedly, maybe too conveniently, Dobbs paid him a visit.

COINCIDENCE NUMBER TWO: They talked for hours.

COINCIDENCE NUMBER THREE: Dobbs is an FBI agent.

COINCIDENCE NUMBER FOUR: THE MOST TROUBLING, THE MOST TELLING: The Professor called during the call-in segment, even though Zack was alerted ahead of time about my not wanting to speak to a Professor Doyle. Yet he put him through, not once, but twice. After hours of conversation with Dobbs, it's hard to believe he didn't recognize the voice. If Doyle is Dobbs, it's hard to believe he didn't know Doyle was Dobbs. Now that's not coincidence."

"How did he explain that, DC?"

"Oh, he hemmed and hawed that Doyle gave him one name the first time and a different name for call two. Also that Doyle must have had two lines open at the same time."

"Why not give him the benefit of the doubt, DC? Maybe he really messed up?"

"Doesn't wash, Jen. How could he hear that voice twice in the space of mere seconds and not recognize it as Brian Dobbs? He had to be in cahoots with Dobbs, or owed him a favor."

"I just can't believe Zack would be in bed with the FBI, Dancy."

"Not the Zack I thought I knew, Jen. Maybe he thought that Dobbs was just fishing around and decided to help an old friend."

"Makes sense, DC. I think."

"Dobbs may not have told him why. If he did, I can't believe Zack would buy into my having anything to do with a right wing group. Not Mr. Liberal DC."

"It's very confusing, Dancy, and I can't get into all those what ifs. All those coincidences. What do we do?"

"For now, nothing. Dobbs and Zack notwithstanding, nobody has a clue about AFTRA, except its members. And they ain't talking. I hope not, anyway."

"Is that a veiled reference to Grace Baldwin?"

"If the shoe fits…In any case, today we're safe. Tomorrow concerns me. Zack concerns me. Even you concern me."

"Why me?"

"Not for what you might do, but for what you know."

"Alright, everyone is on your hit list. What's next?"

"I'll put my brain to work, and work out some kind of trap for Zack to reveal what he knows, what he thinks he knows. And hopefully what he doesn't know."

"Be careful, DC. That might just backfire."

"Well aware of that, but that's for tomorrow, Miss Cabot. Now my brain defers to my stomach. It's time to enjoy this repast fit for the King of Radio."

"Obviously modesty is not your strong suit your majesty!"

"Obviously. So be a nice Queen and pour me another glass of this marvelous claret, and spoon another portion of those silky-smooth garlic mashed potatoes on the Royal plate."

"How can you think of eating at a time like this? I have knots in my stomach."

"I do too, Boston lady, but I call them hunger pains. Warm up the soufflé, I'm almost ready for dessert."

"In the oven, your Royal Highness. However that's not the end to this dinner. There's a special after-dinner treat that I was taught to serve at Harvard."

"What could that be?"

"It's served in the bedroom. Eat up. Quickly."

"Good morning, DC. I came in early to talk about today's show, but really do apologize for screwing up the call-in screening yesterday. I didn't sleep well last night."

"No need to apologize, Zacko. That's yesterday's news. Just don't let it happen again. Right? Have a donut. These Krispy Kremes are delicious. Holes and all."

"Have them every morning, DC. Sometimes just the holes. Janice says they're all going to waist. At least two inches in the past six months. I'll make coffee, though. Want your regular?"

"None for me Zolo. I'm off the stuff for now."

"Zolo? You never called me Zolo before. How now?"

"Seemed like a good idea to save extra syllables not having to say Zoltowski. Does it bother you?"

"No…er…not really. Well a bit. I used to use ZOLO when I applied for a job with a company that didn't hire Jews. Thought I could fake 'em out. It didn't work. Guess my nose and my horns gave me away. Interviewing for this job at WTOP, I decided not to delude anyone about my Jewishness. The station owner being Jewish influenced my brave decision."

"Sorry if I opened up some old wounds, Zack. Won't happen again. For the record, though, the nose I can see. Not the horns."

"Oh, I'm okay with it now. You just caught me by surprise. Any marching orders about today's show, DC?"

"Yeah, something a little different. First off there'll be no call-in segment. We'll give it a rest for awhile."

"Hell, DC, I hope I didn't ruin a good thing for the show?"

"Let's drop the subject. Now about today's show. I want to devote the entire two hours to the Chairman of the Board, Francis Albert Sinatra. Almost a retrospective of his career. What do you think?"

"Super idea. Songs he recorded as the boy singer with Dorsey and James, and then segue to those great hits with great arrangements by Don Costa and Nelson Riddle. Then the Vegas era. It'll show the change in style from the skinny, mellow crooner, to the sophisticated swinger of the rat-pack legend. Neat, DC. Very neat."

"Exactly what I had in mind, Zack. I guess working together these past years you know what's on my mind. You know who I am and what I am."

"I hope so."

"Not too much though. There are some things Dancy Carter wants to keep to himself. Get cracking. Put the list together and let me see it before air time. I need to prepare my intros."

"On it. See you in less than an hour."

"Hold up for a minute, Zack. I need your help on something personal."

"Shoot, boss man."

"You mentioned having an old friend who was high up in the FBI, right?"

"Yeah, Brian Dobbs. What about him?"

"I'm being harassed at home, on the air and in any number of other ways by someone who calls himself Professor Bartholomew Doyle. He professes to teach Political Science at Boston College. I checked him out, and you know what, there's no Professor Doyle on staff at B.C."

"Isn't he the one you told me not to put through during the call-in segment?"

"I think so. He's obviously not who he says he is and his harassment is starting to wear on me. Crank calls from people at odds with my views are what the call-ins are all about. This guy Doyle is far different. He keeps hinting that I'm involved with some white supremacist secret group. If it wasn't funny, it would be tragic."

"DC a right winger? That's like saying Jesse Jackson is a KU KLUX KLAN GRAND DRAGON posing as an activist for the blacks. How can my friend Dobbs help?"

"Not sure. I don't know how the Bureau works, but maybe he can investigate this Doyle guy. He's been calling me at home and only a few, including you, have my unlisted number. Some friends have been approached about my political activities. He's even hinted that Jennifer Cabot and I are having an affair. I suspect he's on a crusade to discredit me. My reputation is at risk, not to mention 'DC ON THE AIR.'"

"What do you want me to do?"

"Arrange a meeting with this FBI friend so I can explore my options as to what can be done to stop him, maybe even find out who the real Doyle is. What do you think?"

"Er…well I…not sure, but I'll ask him. Anything to help, DC. However, he's a busy guy who works out of Boston. I don't know if he has jurisdiction to track down someone in Washington."

"Not Washington, Zack. This Doyle character professes to be from the Boston area. If so, it might be easier for your FBI friend to get a handle on him. If he is your friend, Dobbs that is, maybe he'll be willing to help out another friend of yours. Make any sense?"

"Yeah, yeah, sense. I'll ask him. If that's it I gotta run. We'll be on the air in an hour. Gotta be sure we have all those Sinatra DCs and put that list together."

"Right you are Zack. As usual. Thanks for lending me your ear. Friends come in handy during a crisis. FBI friends for sure. Grab another donut."

"Brian, it's not working. DC has figured out that Professor Doyle is Dobbs, the FBI agent. If you want to smoke out the information about that secret society, find a different approach. One that isn't so obvious.."

"What's the matter, are you losing your nerve?"

"I haven't lost a thing. I don't have to be a rocket scientist to know he has you figured out."

"Don't believe it for one minute. He only thinks he's figured it out. There's doubt. Lots of doubt. Life is simpler for him to think that I'm the professor."

"He's not a simple man, Brian, and what I understand is that your logic is tortured."

"I'm sorry, what you don't understand is that he can't figure out what I really know about that secret society. What I'm going to do with the information I might have that connects him with the group. Information that can destroy his world. Doubt? There's plenty alright, enough to lead him to make mistakes."

"Doubt or no doubt. Your approach is doubtful. Why can't the Bureau use the entire resources it has to probe the group. You have an informant. Why not push him harder? Investigate rather than fake being somebody else to get Carter's mind churning and turning. It puts him on alert to what you're doing. He can see what's coming. Figure out a way to keep him from knowing where you're going. His antenna is way up."

"Don't matter. We're gonna fuzzy up his picture. We're very smart."

"He's smarter. Perceptive, too. Arrogant to a fault, but believes he can outwit your puerile attempt at deception. He'll have your lunch."

"I'll skip lunch."

"I'm not laughing."

"Jokes aside, you've hit the nail squarely on the head. Arrogance. That's his flaw."

"Or his strength."

"No. The man is so caught up in his own ego that he's blinded to the whole picture."

"Yeah, and you're deaf and dumb, Dobbs."

"I don't think so. I think he's running scared. Frightened about his career, his celebrity and the good life that's threatened."

"Let's not play semantics. I can't be part of your fun and games anymore. I work with DC and know he has you pegged."

"Maybe yes, maybe no."

"It's definitely yes. He's on his guard and it's created a siege mentality. He suspects me. His next door neighbor. The boy that delivers the donuts. Everybody."

"Perfect. Exactly what I hoped would happen. Keeps him guessing. Confused. Paranoid. Suspecting everyone. Questioning who are his friends, who are his enemies."

"How long have you been a psychology expert?"

"Not me. The Bureau has experts who use this tool effectively."

"Look Brian, this is going nowhere. Fast, too. I also don't think we should discuss this over the telephone at the station. The walls have ears."

"What do you have in mind?"

"Someplace safe where we can work out a better strategy. One that keeps me out of the loop without a bull's-eye on my back."

"You're right. Can't let that happen. Where?"

"My place after 10 PM."

"Should I bring a bottle of wine, Jennifer?"

"No. Nothing. And don't expect to stay overnight. We may have had something in the past, but there's no present. Or future. I'm not strong enough mentally to have two lovers at the same time."

"We had something good. Didn't we, Jen?"

"For you anyway. It's different now. Carter has a built-in-sensor about things like this. It's almost impossible to fool him."

"Does that mean you'd like to give it another shot?"

"That's not what I mean. If he has a scintilla of doubt about our lovemaking, or that somebody else is in the picture, everything will blow up in our face. Right now I'm a member in good standing with his AFTRA. He trusts me and confides in me. He loves me and I truly love him. No room for anyone else."

"Why then did you throw your hat in with me?"

"Not really sure. Except, I don't advocate overthrowing the government and destroying the Constitution."

"Why then for God's sake did you join up with him?"

"I was sold on the idea that White America is Right America. I was deaf to everything else."

"Thank God you're hearing better now. Has he said anything about the people at AFTRA? Top guys running it, I mean."

"Sort of. In one of our pillow sessions he indicated he's only the lead guy in Washington, but not the leader of the group."

"Who is?"

"Didn't say. Just that somebody big is at the top, pulling the strings, allocating the money, and appointing people to carry out specific assignments. That's the person the Bureau should be targeting. Not DC. Find him and down comes AFTRA like a house of cards."

"I need more, Jen. Something concrete. Anything."

"All I know is that he's powerful. And the money barely touches his hands. It's secreted away in off-shore banks. Millions, Brian. Multi millions. Follow that money trail and you'll find Mr. X. See you later. Remember after 10 PM."

"Jennifer, you know I still love you. Always will. However, I'm not trying to get back in your life just to get Dancy Carter and his un-American radical group. Please know that."

"Don't go there, Mr. Dobbs. I not only don't believe you, but I'm not interested. Not in the least. There was a black cloud hanging over us the last time…your wife and kids. As far as I know they are still there."

"Jen, I'm thinking—"

"Don't Jen me, Mr. Dobbs. Let's not mix your lust with my loyalty to my country. I have some information you want, but you have nothing that gets my motor running. End of that conversation. One other thing, though. Don't tell Zack Zoltowski about our relationship, past or present. Promise on that."

"I promise. Just know that Zack is with me all the way."

"Don't be so sure. That once an agent always an agent thing might not hold up. Zack knows where his bread is buttered. 'DC ON THE AIR' is his baby, too. And he gets a vicarious thrill basking in DC's celebrity. If push came to shove, he would stick with DC in a D.C. minute."

"We'll see, Jennifer. 10 PM."

Dear Mr. Zoltowski (ZOLO):

    I am writing to you as a patriotic American with facts about the man you work with. Dancy Carter is bent on destroying the basic tenets that our founding fathers laid down in the Constitution.

    It makes no difference who I am. I will explain that later. However, I have been a faithful listener to "DC ON THE AIR" for a long time. Usually in agreement with Mr. Carter's commitment to the right causes. (The left ones of course.) I must tell you that Dancy Carter is not the person he purports to be. Behind that liberal mask is the face of a radical right winger who believes White America is Right America.

    Mr. Carter plays a leading role in a secret society with a membership of high-profile men and women from all walks of public and private life, who are committed to changing the many faces of America to one where white is the only color that counts.

    This is a dangerous man you sit beside every day, because he has cleverly infiltrated the hearts and minds of thousands of listeners who believe he champions the causes of the underdog. Myself included. Carter was our rebel with a cause...the do-gooder who would fight the good fight every day. The fight against those special interest people with self-interest as their only interest. In reality he is an evil-no-gooder. How do I know that Mr. Carter is not who he seems to be? And that this secret society does exist? I know because I was one of them for a short while. I was led to believe that I was joining a group dedicated to championing the same causes I believed in. If Dancy Carter was for it, I was for it.

How wrong I was. I was bamboozled by his charm and silvery tongue and taken for a $200,000 ride. Deceived to say the least. I learned in quick order that Carter was espousing something quite different: that White America was in danger of losing its identity to the many colors of the rainbow.

I was appalled and embarrassed and left the group fearing that my reputation would be tarred with that same right wing brush. I could not go public with what I knew or even to the authorities, because I would have had to admit that I was part of a radical group. Not good for my business. More important I did not have proof that the group existed. There was no membership list. No organizational chart. No paper trail. No corporate registration. Nothing that linked Carter to the group.

I am writing to you because I believe you can expose the man and his secret society, since you have the investigative expertise due to your previous life as a top FBI agent. Yes, Mr. Zolo. I know about your years in the Bureau and your inglorious termination.

I don't know if you knew that your former partner, and "friend" Brian Dobbs, betrayed your trust by framing you and causing that ignominious termination. It was his completely false story that you were drunk on the job the night of a surveillance of a key drug lord. This triggered the action of the Director to summarily terminate you. Added to the Bureau's embarrassment was that the drug lord escaped arrest. If you question the truthfulness of any of this, I suggest you request a copy of Dobbs' testimony before the Disciplinary Board of the Bureau. The Freedom of Information Act will enable you to get the document. I did. This information is not meant to open up past old wounds, but to open your eyes about Dobbs' role in your termination, and to establish my credibility. Dobbs is not your friend now and wasn't back then. His reason for getting back in your life is purely self-serving. He wants Carter and the group and doesn't care who gets hurt along the way. This means you and your job. You are just a pawn.

No matter what the situation with Dobbs, it is also imperative that you find a way to stop the egomaniacal, dangerous Dancy Carter from carrying out his plans to change the face of America. I'm sure you can do it without having to get in bed with the treacherous Dobbs and the Bureau.

Zolo, think about it. Think real hard. Know who your friends are, and watch your back against your enemies...posing as friends. Don't be taken in by the *patriotic palaver of an agent with an agenda, or the silver tongue of Dancy Carter.*

If I am able to gather more concrete information, more corroboration about Carter's group, I will write again.

- A CONCERNED AMERICAN

The letter was delivered by a private courier. There were no identifying marks on the envelope. No return address. No signature on the letter. The courier had no idea who was the sender. He was stopped while riding his bike, by a young boy, given a $10 tip, and told to deliver it to no one but a Mr. Zack Zoltowski at radio station WTOP.

Zack couldn't believe his eyes. He read the letter three times, hoping each time that none of what was written was true. He felt utter despair. His value system, his trust of friends, his future, his world was crumbling all around him.

Dobbs had betrayed him in his former life as an agent. A life that one time gave him meaningful purpose. And now DC was betraying his faith in everything he deemed to be sacred. Where could he turn? Who could he turn to? Should he believe anything in the letter? Or was this some sort of prank?

He thought back to his termination by the Bureau, and realized that he had a sneaky suspicion that Dobbs had a hand in that black event. Only Dobbs knew about his drinking. He just could never bring himself to believe that a fellow agent, a partner, a friend, who he spent more time with each day than with his wife and family, could ever betray him. Why? What was his motive? What did he have to gain?

And what was DC's motive in playing the liberal card out in the open, and keeping the cards close to his vest being part of a right wing radical group? What did he have to gain? It was obvious what he had to lose. Is there a gene gone astray in his genetic makeup? Is there a huge sum of money that he could tap into? Is he just the front man or the top dog of the group? Is he angry about something, or has he lost his marbles temporarily? Or maybe, just maybe, your run-of-the-mill evil man. Bigoted, too.

Questions! Questions! Lots of questions. Not many answers. The letter answered some of them. Now it was his turn to answer back. He knew what had to be done. Buy into what Dobbs was selling at least for now, or until Carter was revealed to be that radical no-gooder. Then find a way to discredit Dobbs with the Bureau. Sweet revenge.

Now for Dancy Carter. He would watch every move. Examine every word he utters. Even those that seem innocent, and yet may have another meaning. Hold his feet to the fire for any bigoted remark. Hopefully make him reveal his true feelings about liberals and that white America is where his allegiance is. And then revel in his fall from grace, from the ladder of celebrity.

For the moment it sounded good if he said it fast, but in reality none of it seemed to satisfy the rage that was building up moment to moment.

There was one other avenue to explore, drastic as it may be. Extermination. Rid the world of two evil men with privileged status in the world, but who wanted to destroy people (friends) and freedom.

Extermination? Where the hell did that come from? Too much FBI indoctrination? Carrying a gun for all those years? And would he really consider putting a gun where his rage was leading him?

He reread the letter one more time.

"Jen! It's DC."

"Which DC is that? The liberal god of the airwaves or the radical right winger?"

"Not funny, Boston lady. Not funny at all."

"Ok. I sense you have something serious to get off your chest."

"I tried to call you last night. No answer. No machine. Out on the town with Mother, I presume?"

"Mother is in Boston. I turned off the phone and went to sleep early. It was a trying day."

"Gee, I might have interrupted Morpheus at work."

"What the hell does that mean?"

"Language, lady proper. Watch your language. I dropped by your apartment building a little after 10 PM, because I thought something was wrong."

"Dropped by my apartment in the late evening? Pray tell what did you think was wrong?"

"You didn't answer the phone, and your answering machine didn't pick up either. I thought that was kinda odd. I was genuinely concerned, since it was only 9:30. I know your evening regimen on work day nights, staying up for the 11:00 news and then reading some Danielle Steele stuff 'til those pretty eyes start to tear up and close."

"I didn't do either last night. And what's more I'm a lot ticked off that you were checking up on me."

"Wrong, love. I wasn't checking up on you, just checking on whether you were ok. Don't ask me why, but I decided to see for myself. That's when I went to Watergate. My concern was genuine, and only grew when your doorman told me some stranger delivered a package to you around 10:00. The man never came down."

"How did you know he never came down?"

"I waited in the lobby about an hour. No sign of a delivery man."

"Did it ever occur to you that the doorman had the wrong apartment number Carter?"

"It did, but that didn't diminish my concern."

"Well for your information, no one delivered a package to me last night. If he did, I didn't hear the bell because I was fast asleep. Also turned off my machine so as not to be disturbed."

"Makes sense, Jen. I'm sure the doorman was confused about the apartment number, and the delivery man was not a delivery man. Probably visiting his girl, on your floor, with a gift of sorts."

"Carter, you're full of it. And I don't appreciate the sarcasm or even what you're implying. Don't patronize me."

"I'm not patronizing you."

"Maybe not, but whatever nonsense you're tossing around sounds accusatory to this Boston lady's well-tuned ears. If there was a man in my apartment, he was entertaining himself. I was in bed alone and fast asleep."

"Sorry, Jen, I apologize if I sound accusatory. I don't mean to. In truth, the green-eyed monster of jealousy grabbed me by the ears. Don't ask me why, but I couldn't kick the idea that you were with another man. Please don't misunderstand, I'm not suggesting that there was another man. It was my mind playing tricks with my ego. Besides that, I don't own you, Jen. Just love you."

"That's big of you. Especially the don't own me part."

"I meant it. Let me make it up to you. Boorish behavior and jealousy. Come to my place tonight. I'll order in a double pepperoni pizza with extra mozzarella, uncork a bottle of the good stuff, and supply some stimulating Jazz. Just got a new release, a remastered CD of Ella Fitzgerald in Berlin. A triple threat evening. Pizza, Ella and me. What do you say?"

"I say that's the height of arrogance. You admit spying on me. Accusing me of being with another man and then have the audacity to invite me to drink and make merry by crawling in bed with you.

That's off the charts, music man. I have other plans. I'm taking the 4 PM shuttle to Boston. Mother is hosting one of her soirees for a long lost cousin. If we're still talking, I'll speak to you on Monday. By the way, if you have nothing special to do, wait outside my building and maybe that mysterious delivery man will finally emerge."

When she hung up, Dancy smiled. That crooked, sardonic smile that women loved. He had touched a nerve. More likely had caught Miss Boston Proper in a rather delicate situation. A late night caller. Very interesting, he thought.

It did bother him a touch, that his undeniable charm and confession of love hadn't kept the society deb from cheating. Hadn't kept her from messing up the sheets with someone else. He had a sneaking suspicion that her hastily arranged trip to Boston for Mama's soiree had more going for it. And the long lost cousin might be an FBI agent named Brian Dobbs.

Makes sense, he thought. Dobbs is a friend of Zack and an FBI agent to boot. Dobbs is from Boston. Jennifer Cabot is from Boston royalty. Did they know each other before? Lovers?

He was perturbed that his Washington bed-mate was going home to get it on again with that Bureau man. Would Dobbs tell her he's Professor Doyle? Would she tell him about AFTRA? Lots happening. Lots of lying and shifting of allegiances. All the key players involved: Blabbermouth Grace Baldwin, Mother Cabot, Jennifer Cabot, Zack Zoltowski. The gang of four. All my friends. Friends? With friends like this, AFTRA doesn't need enemies. Doesn't need the FBI to take it apart, it's being disemboweled from within by friends.

He dialed Mr. B's private number.

"Hi folks, DC back with you on WTOP 1500 on your AM dial. The station where Washingtonians turn on to 'DC ON THE AIR', to be turned on by the music they want when they want it.

That last song, 'Sarah,' was sung by the incredibly gifted Carmen McRae, also on the piano. Miss McRae wrote the song as a personal eulogy to her life-long friend, Sarah Vaughan. Sassy to her friends and the Divine One to her fans, Miss McRae wrote this haunting song shortly after Sarah Vaughan passed away. It's a remarkable tribute to her and the many other Jazz divas that passed on before her.

Well, I'm sorry to say, but we're coming up to the moment of truth every Monday through Friday on WTOP 1500 on your AM dial. That's when the inexorable hour hand is approaching 3:00 PM. The time for DC to bid goodbye to D.C. land. See you on Monday, same place WTOP 1500 on your AM dial, same time 1:00 PM. But you know that.

By the way, for all you political buffs out there, we'll be reinstating our popular call-in segment on Monday at 2:00 PM. Lots to talk about. Hope you have lots of questions and comments. So clear your minds and sharpen your pencils. Speak to you then. Goodbye Mrs. B.

Take us out Zack with a little bit of Sarah Vaughan and 'Don't Blame Me'."

"Nice show, DC. Good stuff on Carmen McRae. Oh, I forgot to mention, that my FBI friend can't make your dinner date tonight."

"How come?"

"An important business function to attend in Boston. However, he does want to meet with you, and will get in touch about next week."

"When did you find out, Zacko?"

"About a half hour ago."

"My, my, must have been an important function to cancel at the 11th hour."

"Must be, but he didn't say what."

"Or with whom, I guess."

"Guess so."

"Thanks anyway. I only hope it's not the typical bureaucratic way of politely saying no."

"No. I don't think so. He sounded sincere. Said it was very important to be in Boston. He'll be in touch next week."

"Thanks again. See you Monday. Shalom Shebat."

"If you feel religion coming on, come to the services this Saturday. The Rabbi's sermon will be interesting."

"How so?"

"It's on Friendship and Loyalty."

"That's timely. However, I have to pass. Meeting with the boss lady at 10 AM. FCC stuff again."

"Oh, she won't be here, DC. Miss Cabot mentioned going to Boston tonight. Some function her mother is hosting."

"This seems to be my unlucky weekend. Everybody has a function in Boston. I seem to be the odd man out in Washington. Oh, well, maybe a little religion will save my grieving soul. See you in Shul. Save a bagel for me."

A bagel for my soul, thought Dancy Carter. Ironic that my brain says that a conspiracy is at work…and it's moving north. Brian Dobbs has a function in Boston. Jennifer Cabot has a soiree in Boston. Is a function different from a soiree? Or does the Bureau man call a soiree a function?

No matter what it's called, it could be a way for the "delivery man" to be with the Boston lady for a second round of the mattress polka. Not to mention a pillow talk discussion about Dancy Carter and AFTRA.

Now his mind was running wild. In every direction. Nothing was funny or something to joke about. Bile was building up rapidly in the back of his throat. He could actually taste it. He spit twice into the sink and poured himself a double shot of Jack Daniels.

He felt he needed something else. Something more satisfying. The chocolate cookie? That seemed very satisfying. He picked up the phone and called her. A little black loving might be the perfect antidote for his black mood.

"Hi, this is DC."

"Does that stand for Damn Crumbun?"

"I deserve that. Can I make amends?"

"What does your devilish mind have in mind?"

"Drinks and dinner at Dukes. A few laughs for old times' sake. Nothing else."

"Nothing else for sure, Mr. Carter. If there is, forget it. Take a cold shower instead."

"Agreed. Pick you up at 8 PM. And I'll take a cold shower, too."

After arranging the date, Carter reflected upon what he had just done. Was it hypocritical to think that maybe, just maybe, Jennifer was cheating on him, while he was definitely going to pursue sex with Miss Black America? Shower or no shower. No doubt, he thought. But rationalization was the operative word. Sex was one thing, but proving that whatever DC wanted, DC could get. That's what mattered.

In the midst of all this convoluted and tortured thinking, the ringing of the phone jarred him back to reality.

"DC, it's Jennifer. And before you can say something funny, I want to be serious and apologize for my earlier behavior."

"No need."

"Yes there is. I was being childish and churlish, and also remiss in not inviting you to Mother's soiree. So I'm inviting you now. Can you come?"

"Is this your idea, Jen, or did Mama push you into it?"

"I thought of it, but Mother pushed me into it."

"That's honest of you to admit. I'm grateful that one of the female members of the Cabot family has the good breeding to invite a common working stiff to an elite social function."

"I've eaten crow, Mr. Carter, so there's no need for sarcasm. The apology still stands. Twice. Once for my boorish, unsocialite behavior and second for not beating my mother to the punch in extending an invitation myself."

"Twice accepted, Boston lady. Regrettably I have to turn you down."

"Still piqued?"

"No. It's not because I'm being spiteful or ungrateful, but I made a previous engagement."

"Anybody I know?"

"Could be. I took your advice and went to Watergate and met someone who delivers things. I was invited to a beer and pizza soiree at a local diner. Can't cancel at this late hour."

"Can't or won't? Too bad. You might have enjoyed talking with Mother's guest of honor...a professor of Political Science at a well-known Boston bastion of higher learning."

They both laughed out loud and hung up simultaneously.

"Mr. Carter? This is Brian Dobbs of the FBI. I hope I'm not interfering with your morning routine. I apologize for having to cancel our appointment on such short notice. When the Bureau calls I have to answer."

"No problem, Mr. Dobbs."

"Our mutual friend Zack Zoltowski said that you do have some sort of problem. Is it Federal or local?"

"Not quite sure, but it is personal and potentially painful to my career and reputation."

"Do you want to talk about it, sir?"

"That's why I asked for this meeting. I most certainly do. Although I have a feeling I've spoken to you before. Your voice sounds quite familiar."

"I doubt that, sir. However, I'll be in Washington for the rest of the day, so if you wish we can meet later. I have meetings until 2 PM, then I'm free."

"Fine Mr. Dobbs. Just fine."

"Please call me Brian. Mr. Dobbs was how they addressed my father. May I call you DC?"

"Why not. Everybody else does, except my father. Today is good. How about 3:30 PM after my show? We can meet at my office at the station."

"Will that be private enough, DC?"

"Sure. Speaking of private, how did you get my private number?"

"I got it…I got it from Zack."

"Heard you were in Boston this weekend. Work or play, Brian?"

"Work, work, work, like most weekends these days. There's no 9 to 5 schedule at the Bureau. Every day is a workday. The weekend is like any weekday. 3:30 would be good for me, DC."

"Excellent. May I buy you dinner for your trouble?"

"That's gracious, DC, but I have to be back in Beantown tonight. I'm booked on the 8 PM shuttle. Maybe some other time. A couple of hours? Does that give us enough time to talk about your problem?"

"More than enough. If you can, come by a few minutes earlier and I'll introduce you to a fellow Bostonian, our Administrative VP, Jennifer Cabot. She's from the Boston Cabots. Zack mentioned you might know her. Maybe at one of those cocktail functions and soirees her mother is famous for."

"I never had the good fortune or pleasure of knowing her or being invited to one of those parties. I do know the Cabot name. Everybody who's anybody in Boston has heard of the Cabots."

"She's a nice lady, Brian."

"Thanks for the thought, DC. Some other time maybe, today I'm tight for time. See you at 3:30."

"Look forward to it, Thanks in advance for taking the time out of a busy schedule protecting our country against those who conspire to undermine our Constitution."

"Yes sir. That's what I do."

"3:30 it is, Brian. I'll leave word at security that you are expected. Although I'm sure an FBI badge is the best kind of ID. See you then."

Come into my web said the spider to the fly, sang Dancy Carter in the most atonal, godforsaken dissonance. He clapped his hands in utter, unrestrained joy at the prospect of meeting Professor Doyle, AKA Brian Dobbs, face to face.

At 3:30 p.m., not 3:31, Agent Dobbs was ushered into Carter's office. The Bureau's penchant for punctuality was intact.

"Mr. Carter...DC."

"Mr. Dobbs...Brian. Have a seat. May I offer you something to drink? Coffee, soda, water, wine, scotch?"

"Never drink on the job, DC."

"Coffee?"

"No, I mean scotch or wine."

"Water then?"

"If you insist. I don't want to seem rude, DC, but I am on a tight schedule, so if you don't mind can we get right to your problem? And why do you believe the Bureau can help you better than the local authorities?"

"Not the Bureau, Brian, but you specifically. Your reputation as a super investigator precedes you. Zack has high praise for your skills."

"He intends to exaggerate a bit."

"Maybe so, but I trust his judgment implicitly. After all he is my producer. In any case, I don't know who does best, Brian. My feeling is that this is something for the FBI. It seems like a jurisdictional issue and the local P.D. is ill-equipped to handle it."

Zack rushed into the office waving a piece of paper.

"DC lookee here. Just received this fax. Oops, I'm sorry, I didn't know you had a visitor. Forgive me for interrupting."

"Hi Zack."

"Brian Dobbs? I didn't know you were seeing Mr. Carter today?"

"Had a few hours to spare, so DC was kind to see me on very short notice."

"What's up," said Carter a little miffed. "What's on the fax?"

"It can wait. I apologize again."

"No, no go ahead. You're here now and we haven't started to talk."

"It's great news, DC, that's why I'm so excited."

"Yeah, yeah. Spill it out Zoltowski."

"This is from Maria Cole, Nat 'King' Cole's wife. She'll be in Washington on Wednesday and wants to meet and present you with an album of the original King Cole Trio, recorded in the early '40s and autographed by the King himself. She says it's in appreciation for playing his records so often and the kind words you always have to say about him. This keeps his name and legacy alive."

"Nice of her. E-mail her back and invite her to be my guest for lunch before the show. Ask if she would be willing to spend some time live on the air. Our listeners will love it."

"Nat 'King' Cole?" said Brian. "Gosh, DC, you do lead an exciting musical life. Zack hit it on the nail when he said you are 'THE MUSIC MAN' in D.C. All us FBI guys do is track down serial killers, bank robbers, the ten worst killers and radical groups. Rarely run into a celebrity without a checkered past."

"Where are you going, Zack?", said DC.

"I thought you wanted a private chat with Dobbs, DC."

"That was before. You're here and you know why we're having this meeting. Stick around. You might have to fill in any of the blanks that I leave out. Do you mind, Brian, if Zack sits in?"

"If it's ok with you, it's ok with me. Another agent mind to maybe solve your problem can't hurt."

"Another agent mind?"

"Oh, I goofed. You didn't know about Zack's past with the Bureau? I won't say another word."

"What the hell is he talking about, Zoltowski?"

"Well I…er…mmm, I used to be with the Bureau a thousand years ago. For the record, I don't have an agent's mindset anymore. My mind is cluttered with musical programming, sponsor commercial breaks, handling your segues and making lousy coffee. Picking up donuts, too."

"Hey, I'm sorry, Zack, if I spoke out of turn."

"No it's alright, Brian. It had to come out sometime. I never told DC about my past. It didn't seem important."

"Well, well. He's a good producer, Brian. Was he a good agent?"

"The top of the top. A great investigator with many commendations, and a sharpshooter to boot. My partner and friend for 10 years."

"How about that! The quiet, religious Zack Zoltowski an FBI agent. A sharpshooter, no less. You devil. This is turning out to be a great meeting without ever getting to my problem."

"Don't wish to be rude, DC, but time is running short. What's your problem?"

"It started some weeks ago when a Professor Doyle called me at home. He said he was a Professor of Political Science at Boston College."

"Was that unusual? The call I mean."

"At first not at all. He took me to task for being against Senator Harris' bill for increased military spending. I politely told him I don't take calls at home, and to call the station during call-in time."

"Nothing special there, DC."

"Then he said he had rock-solid information that I knew something about a radical right wing group in Washington. I told him unequivocally I didn't have a clue as to what he was talking about."

"What's the problem?"

"My sense was that he was linking me with the group. I was also very suspicious of someone, anyone on the outside calling me on my unlisted private number. Only close friends have the number. I hung up."

"Good move."

"However, I was disturbed that he was attempting to link me with a radical group, so I checked out the professor. There was no Professor Doyle at Boston College."

"Did that solve your problem, or is there more?"

"I felt he would call during the show, ask the same questions, with the intent to embarrass me on the air. I told Zack to screen any calls from Professor Doyle. He got through. Not once, but twice."

"Yeah, it was my fault. I goofed Brian. I embarrassed DC. It could have cost me my job. He gave me a break, chewed me out, but I wasn't fired."

"That was a nice thing to do, DC. However, I don't see any real problem yet."

"Oh, there's more. Doyle called friends, many of my charity contacts, people at the station, hinting not so subtly, that I was involved in a plot to radicalize the political process in Washington. That my liberal face was a false one."

"It's getting more interesting, DC."

"Think about it, Brian. If this Doyle guy was given any air time he could have poisoned the minds of my listeners."

"I understand. Tell me what you want the Bureau to do?"

"I'm not really sure whether it's the Bureau or just you. Boyle is not a professor of anything, but is a professional troublemaker. Dangerous, in my view. Maybe he's into blackmail, extortion or some other illegal venture."

"Maybes don't make it a Federal crime, DC, more like a local civil suit possibility. So where do I come in?"

"For starters, he used Boston College. Maybe he is from Boston. You operate out of Boston and you may have a file on someone who makes false accusations against public figures. Maybe that constitutes a Federal crime: blackmail, wire fraud, extortion, illegal use of the mails or airwaves. Hey, I have no idea what I'm talking about, Brian, but would hope the bureau takes a dim view of this."

"We certainly do. And we do have dossiers on many of these wild-eyed malcontents."

"Look at it this way, Brian, if Doyle threatens me he could do the same to other public figures. And the public will surely lose faith in those public or political people who advocate one stance and practice another."

"I get your point. I believe it's a valid point. And yes, if he is part of an organized group using airwaves, the postal service and other communication vehicles to spew his venom, it's possible the Bureau would investigate."

"That's encouraging, Brian. At least it's a start."

"Maybe, but maybe not. I'll put my best computer agent on it. If we can find out anything about a Professor Bartholomew Doyle, or someone who fits that profile, I'll move to the next step. How's that?"

"Can't ask for more, Brian. Now how about that drink?"

"Some other time. I do have to run or the plane might leave without me. See you partner. Keep in touch."

"Cool it, Dobbs, I'm not your partner anymore."

"Sorry about that, Zack. It's tough to break old habits. Glad we got together, DC. I will try to help, but don't expect too much."

"Oh, you've helped a great deal already. Thanks for coming in Agent Dobbs. Brian."

"DC, we have to talk."

"Jen, I'm on the air now. If it's something important talk fast, I'm in a 90 second commercial break."

"No, we have to do some serious talking that'll take much longer than 90 seconds. Let's do it later after you go off the air. Privately."

"My office, Jen? Or my place? Or maybe yours?"

"My place."

"Will you be wearing a wire for your FBI friend?"

"I deserve that, DC. But I won't be wired. You can strip search me if that will satisfy you."

"Now you're talking, Boston lady. A strip search would be most satisfying. However, I'm not too sure we'd ever get around to serious talking. Heavy breathing more likely."

"No jokes, please."

"You didn't mention a bug in the lamp or the coffee table, Jen. Or in the clock over the mantel. Will I have to face one of those locations and speak directly at it?"

"Don't make this a farce, DC. No wires, no bugs. No nothing but serious talk. I swear on my father's grave."

"That's serious. What time?"

"Any time after 7 PM."

"Should I bring a pizza and a bottle of wine? Or is this just really serious talk time? Girlo to mano?"

"Serious talk time, DC. No pizza, no wine. An empty stomach and a clear head will keep us focused. Me for sure."

"After 7 PM it is. I'll be wearing a red carnation, so please notify your doorman that the guy wearing the red carnation is delivering something to apartment 4B."

"Don't be cruel, DC. I get your not so subtle humor. Please try to be serious, because I am. Dead serious."

"Forgive me. I couldn't resist that little jab, but I realize that you're really serious about being serious. No more one-liners. Seriously."

"DC!"

"See you later, boss lady."

FOUR HOURS LATER: JENNIFER CABOT'S APARTMENT

"Right on time, Dancy. I appreciate that. Forgive me if I seem a bit nervous."

"Not any more than I am, Jen."

"Make yourself comfortable on the couch while I change into something more comfortable. Not a teddy or anything sexy. Just a plain old-lady robe."

"I'm sure it's a sexy old-lady robe."

"Carter?"

"I'll try, Jen. I promise."

"Sit down, the couch is not bugged. I told you no wires or listening devices. Trust me."

"Trust you?"

"Alright, alright. I know I'm going to eat a lot of crow tonight, so give me the benefit of the doubt. Trust me. Believe me."

"Done. I believe you. What's the topic of this serious talk?"

"Give me a minute to change."

In a few minutes Jennifer returned wearing a bulky chenille robe.

"Hey, that's a nice old-lady robe. Very proper for a proper Boston lady to get everything off her chest."

"Dancy, please."

"Right. Serious. Okay, I'm ready."

"Dancy, I lied to you. I knew Brian Dobbs from my deb days. We dated. We were lovers. One of my many flings, whether the guy was married or not. He wanted to marry me. A short time later he said he couldn't leave his wife because of the kids."

"Would you have married him?"

"Yes. But I broke it off immediately. When I spoke to him recently he told me about using the Professor Doyle alias to harass you. I gave him your private number even though I knew he was FBI."

"Why?"

"I don't really know."

"Don't know or you won't tell? Sorry, go ahead."

"He was the delivery man the other night. Nothing happened, though."

"Nothing?"

"Nothing sexual. We talked about the past. He said he still loved me. Then he got around to you. How he pushed a button about a right wing group. Asked if I knew anything, and I blabbed a bit about AFTRA...and your role in it."

"A little bit would mean a lot to an FBI agent. The question is why? You're part of it. Why even admit there was an AFTRA?"

"Don't interrupt, DC. Hear me out. Brian caught me in a moment of weakness about still loving me and wanting to get back again. I lost focus. So I blabbed."

"Would you get back with him again?"

"No. Then I realized I had made a serious mistake."

"Dear lady, that's the understatement of understatements."

"I told him in no uncertain terms that I loved you."

"I hate to think what else you would have told him if you hated me."

"You must try and understand, DC. Dobbs told me his marriage was on the rocks. His job in jeopardy. You were his last chance to maybe salvage both. I fell for the crocodile tears. I felt sorry for him. I guess my maternal instincts got the better of me."

"You've never been a mother, Jen."

"Bite your tongue, DC. Hard. And listen. I tried to end the conversation, but stupidly compounded the situation by inviting him to Mother's social. She was ecstatic. Dobbs was more her cup of tea than Dancy Carter. He was Boston society, and with his impending divorce would be a perfect match for her precious daughter. A match that Boston's elite would welcome."

"You'd actually marry him?"

"No, of course not. But that didn't matter to her. Even though she bought into AFTRA lock, stock and barrel, a society marriage is where she lives. Commoner Carter wasn't the right man for her society daughter."

"I'm biting hard, Jen. Real hard."

"I'm almost through, Dancy, then you can put my feet to the fire. Or put me on the rack."

"How did AFTRA get into the conversation with him?"

"Mother asked him what he knew. He said very little except what his informant leaked, as vague as that was. A little bit more when I confirmed it existed. And a lot more when I mentioned that you were a major player."

"That really clinched the deal for him, eh, Jen?"

"Bite, DC. Then Mother surprised the hell out of me by asking him to forget what he heard or knew, and back off investigating you. Marrying me was ok, but AFTRA was off limits."

"Then what?"

"That AFTRA and Dancy Carter were good for the Cabots and White America. That the FBI was a dead-end career for someone married to her daughter. Even hinting, that a good paying position would be available in a Cabot enterprise."

"Don't tell me he turned her down?"

"He did. I never thought he had the balls to refuse mother. He said his private life wasn't for sale, and his Bureau life could never be compromised. That he took an oath to protect the Constitution."

"That was noble, Miss Cabot, but understandable. He had a mouse in his trap."

"Well, his no meant no Jennifer. Mother was furious and told him to leave. I was furious, not because Dobbs turned me down, but because my dear mother never even asked me if I wanted him in my life."

"I'm getting more furious by the second, Miss Boston. Are you through?"

"Almost. Just one more thing. Dobbs told me that Zack new everything about AFTRA and was on board to take you down."

"I've bitten through my tongue, Miss Cabot. Are you finished?"

"I believe so."

"That was the worst bunch of romantic gibberish you just laid on me, lady. Now what was the real reason for telling Dobbs about AFTRA."

"You're not going to believe me Dancy."

"Probably not, but try me."

"I wanted AFTRA to be destroyed to save you."

"That's the most tortured reasoning I ever heard."

"See! I knew you wouldn't buy it."

"Buy it? I would have to be on a different planet to buy it. How could I be saved with AFTRA being destroyed? Do you have some special vanishing cream to have me blend in with the woodwork? Did you think for one minute if AFTRA was exposed that Dancy Carter would be invisible?"

"It was brain lock, DC. I was for the basic premise that White America is Right America, but was troubled about over-throwing the government. Changing the Constitution. I love my country and couldn't bear the idea of destroying the great experiment called Democracy."

"What the hell are you babbling about?"

"No need to swear, Mr. Carter. I'm trying desperately to be civilized."

"Civilized. You took an oath to be part of AFTRA. You betrayed that oath, yet accuse me of betraying the country. How can you mention civilized in the light of that? Did it ever dawn on you if AFTRA was brought down along with me that you, your mother and her friends would take the fall, too? What were you thinking?"

"I guess I wasn't. The truth is I'm still with you, and so is Mother and her friends."

"Great to hear. That solves everything, but one little, inconsequential thing. How do we prevent Dobbs from knowing what he knows? How do you unring the bell you rung, Cabot?"

"I don't know, DC. I only hope no one heard the bell."

"Naïve, lady. It was heard. Loud and clear, and he has enough information to put a full court press on me and put AFTRA in mothballs. Maybe putting me in Leavenworth."

"I don't think so. He can't get you out in the open so easily."

"Wrong. There's no place for me to hide. Even if I avoid prison, my world will be over. No career. No status in liberal causes. Hypocrite will be the kindest word to describe me."

"Real friends will stand by you."

"Like Zack? God only knows what he will do now that he's reupped as an agent."

"What's the answer, DC? Do you have something in mind?"

"You're not going to like it, dear lady, but you've forced my hand. Only one course to take."

"Whatever that means, Dancy, it sounds ominous."

"Ominous, yes. More like draconian. They have to be eliminated if AFTRA is to stay whole. And ditto for me."

"This is a joke, right DC? Funning at my expense. Just scaring the hell out of me for goofing up."

"No joke. I'm dead serious. As serious as you wanted our talk to be. I have no choice. Everything is at stake, and dire circumstances call for drastic action."

"Come on, DC, you're not a killer. You're a disc jockey with mixed up politics. You got yourself into this fix and can get out of it by simply disbanding AFTRA."

"Disbanding my dream?"

"Sometimes you have to destroy a dream to save reality. Dobbs doesn't have any hard evidence. You can live with the rumors."

"Sounds good if you say it fast, Jen, but it's too late. Projects are moving ahead. People are involved. We can't turn back."

"Nonsense. You run the operation and you can abort everything. Without your leadership, AFTRA dies."

"I don't run AFTRA. I'm just a front man because of my celebrity. An important biggie is the leader. He calls the shots (forgive the pun). Controls the money. Plans the plan. Has the political clout."

"It's never too late, DC."

"The train has left the station, Jen. We all boarded the same train. We're on a fast track to our destination. We can't put the brakes on this express train."

"A brilliant, but tortured metaphor, lover. I just don't give a damn what track the train is on, you can't mean murder. That's not the man I know and love. It must be the MAN himself."

"No, that's exactly what I mean. I, we have no options."

"I can't buy that, Dancy. Please listen. Get out of AFTRA. Play your music, don't play politics anymore. Go on with your life as the ultimate do-gooder."

"Sorry, Boston lady. The die is cast. They die or yours truly is as good as dead himself. Not letting you off the hook for what you did, Jen, I still want you with me. Can I count on that?"

"Why must it come down to do or die?"

"For the last time, Jen, then our serious talk is over. You opened your big mouth, which has created a chain reaction. I am up to my armpits in FBI agents who want to tear off my arms and toss the rest of my body to the wolves. I don't relish the idea, but it must and will be done. Answer me. Are you still with me?"

"Yes. But this is wrong, Dancy. I beg you to find another way out."

"I don't think I can on an empty stomach, dear lady. I'm starved. Put on some clothes and we'll have dinner at Dukes. The usual: Crabmeat cocktail, a healthy cut of prime rib and a vintage year of Chateau Petrus. I'm dead serious, Jen."

"About Dobbs and Zack?"

"No. About dinner. Get dressed."

"Hey D.C., DC, Dancy Carter is back with you all on WTOP 1500 on your AM dial. It's 1:51 PM and at the top of the hour Jack and Jill Boyd will update all the news. And Bill Brown will give us the business report of the day.

Right now it's a brisk 39 degrees. The sun is shining brightly, but doing very little to keep the chill from running up and down your spine. Don't despair. DC will warm you up quickly. Musically that is.

For those of you stranded on a deserted island for a long period of time, that last song was 'Straighten Up and Fly Right' by the original King Cole Trio. It was recorded in the early '40s. So now keep tuned in to 'DC ON THE AIR' on WTOP, 1500 on your AM dial. Why, you ask? Glad you asked. There's going to be more of King Cole after the break.

But first, the surprise I hinted at earlier. A beautiful surprise it is, too. Sitting at my side is the beautiful lady who was always at the side of Nat "King" Cole. His wife Maria.

"Welcome to 'DC ON THE AIR,' Mrs. Cole."

"Thank you for inviting me, Mr. Carter."

"No, no. No Mr. Carter. Just DC."

"Fine then. No more Mrs. Cole. Just Maria."

"Deal lady. First let me thank you for your generous gift of the first album ever recorded by the King Cole Trio. Autographed too."

"My pleasure, DC. It's a token, a small one, of my appreciation for your playing Nat's records so often. Nat loved DJ's. Kept his name and music in front of the listening and record-buying public. Kept his records riding high on the charts. He always felt without their support, he would have been just another piano player."

"Not on your life, Maria. We may have played his records, but our loyal listeners recognized his genius. They asked us to play him. And his talent was too huge for him to ever be just another piano player. Not to mention his incredible singing voice."

"Maybe so, DC. But you and other DJ's from coast to coast played his songs when he was alive, and now are keeping his legacy alive long after he's passed. I'm grateful."

"That's the least we can do. Our listeners demand it. I get requests every day to play more King Cole records. That's the hallmark of a great artist."

"Thank you, sir. My family thanks you."

"Folks, in case you forgot, you're listening to 'DC ON THE AIR' on WTOP 1500 on your AM Dial with my surprise guest Maria Cole, the late Nat 'King' Cole's wife. Thanks for being here, Maria.

Now I have another surprise for all you music lovers out there in D.C. land, and for Maria Cole. I'll be playing a half hour of King Cole's most famous recordings without commercial interruption. How's that grab you? All the songs were selected by you in a call-in vote. Maria can you stay with us for those thirty minutes?"

"Love to, DC."

"This is DC, Dancy Carter with 'DC ON THE AIR' on WTOP 1500 on your AM Dial. It's coming up on 2 PM, so we'll break for the news and the business report. When we return it'll be a trip down memory lane with Nat 'King' Cole and the lovely Maria Cole sitting right next to DC. We'll lead off with his famous recording of Mona Lisa."

That brought a nice smile to Maria Cole's face.

"Cue us up, Zack."

* * *

The story was tucked away on page 36 of the Washington Post, in small type, about the tragic death of FBI agent Brian Dobbs, a member of a prominent Boston society family. According to official initial reports, Dobbs fish-tailed on a rain-slickened road just minutes from his Boston suburban home and crashed into a concrete abutment. He died instantly.

In the offices of Jennifer Cabot and Zack Zoltowski it was as if the story was in 72 point headline type on the front page.

Cabot rushed into Dancy Carter's office and screamed at the top of her lungs, "You bastard! You did it. You're a murderer."

"Hold your horses, Miss Cabot. What did I do? And who the hell did I murder?"

"Don't play games with me. You know exactly what I'm talking about. And who. It's in the Post. Brian Dobbs was killed driving his car into an abutment near his home in Boston."

"I haven't read the Post, yet, however it sounds like Dobbs had an accident. How did you conclude he was murdered…much less by me? You said it happened in Boston? Well I haven't been out of Washington."

"Now you're making light of the situation, Mr. Carter. You said elimination and that's what happened to Brian. He was conveniently eliminated in an accident-style murder."

"An accident-style murder? That's an odd choice of words. And aren't you jumping to conclusions? Have the authorities ruled it suspicious? If not, what makes you think it was murder?"

"You wanted him dead and he's dead. An accident that stinks-to-high-heaven of murder."

"There you go again, Cabot. You must be smoking some strong stuff. How do I make a murder turn into an accident? I just play records. I'm not a magician."

"Okay, so maybe you didn't pull the trigger."

"Pull the trigger? I thought he died in a car crash?" "You know damn well what I mean, Carter. You didn't personally take part in whatever made Brian's car smash into that cement wall. You know who did. Maybe even ordered it. More important we both know why."

"You're way off base, Miss Cabot. If and when the police determine there was foul play involved, then you can spew all the ill-advised accusations you want. Until then back off. Go back to your office. I have a show to prepare for."

"This is the end of our relationship, Carter. I can't live with the thought that someone I slept with, and loved, could be a monster. I hope you can sleep well tonight, Dancy Carter."

"I sleep remarkably sound, Miss Cabot, especially when I sleep alone."

* * *

Shortly after Jennifer Cabot left his office, the hunched figure of Zack Zoltowski opened the door without knocking. His face was ashen white, but his eyes were black with hate. He kept one hand in his jacket pocket. Carter was startled to see Zack walking slowly towards him. Before he could say anything, Zack pulled out a gun and pointed it at Carter's head.

"What the hell are you doing, Zack? Have you lost control of your senses?"

"You killed him you two-faced, right-wing bastard. And I'm going to blow your head off."

"Are you out of your mind? I didn't kill anybody. Jennifer Cabot just told me that Brian Dobbs died in a car crash. Do you think for one minute I had anything to do with an accident? An accident!"

"You bet I do. Jennifer told me about your plan to eliminate him."

"Come on, Zack, that was just talk in the heat of the moment. Killing is not what I do. I just play records."

"Sure, and a Mafia Don just sits at the head of his table."

"What the hell does that mean? If anything, you should be pointing that gun at yourself."

"And what does that mean, Carter?"

"You have as good a reason to get rid of him as anyone, just to get even for his lying that got you run out of the Bureau."

"That was ten years ago, and I don't hold a grudge that long."

"Maybe so, but if anyone has the know-how to make a murder look like an accident, you've got the credentials."

"Great stuff, Dancy Carter. The best defense is a good offense. You had every reason to want Dobbs dead. And I have every reason to make you pay for it."

"Put that gun down, Zack, or else you'll be making a mistake that will haunt you forever."

"I'll be haunted if I don't do something."

"I know what you and Dobbs were up to, trying to link me with some right wing group. He had nothing on me, except suspicion. He couldn't arrest me on suspicion, so why would I think of killing him? Furthermore, all you know about me and that group is what he told you. He lied about you before, why not lie to you now?"

"He wasn't lying."

"No? Cabot told me how desperate he was to save his career, just like back then with you. So he set about bringing down a high-profile celebrity. Namely yours truly. He sucked you in Zack because it served his own interests."

"He had proof, Carter. The Cabots. Their friends. Others. And was very close to nailing the guy who gave you your orders."

"What guy? Orders about what? It's pure hogwash."

"You're a pathological liar as well, Dancy. I have a letter from someone who was part of your right wing group. He got out, but he spelled out in chapter and verse your involvement. It's solid proof."

"His name, Zack, what's his name?"

"He wanted to protect his identity and signed it 'a concerned American.'"

"No name? Solid proof? In a pig's eye. I can give you a more logical take on the letter. It's not from any concerned American. I believe it was your partner Dobbs."

"Dobbs?"

"Makes all the sense in the world. Remember his clumsy Professor Doyle attempt to discredit me? Writing a letter and not signing it smacks of another clumsy attempt to smear me."

"Why would he do that, Carter?"

"Simple. To make you believe he was giving you facts from a very reliable source. Someone who was on the inside, but conveniently got out."

"Why go to all that trouble, Dancy?"

"Ten years. Ten years to salve a guilty conscience for his lying about you to the Bureau. Think about it. It obviously worked, since you forgot about his deceit and threw your lot in with him. Now I suggest that you put that gun down and come to your senses, before I call security and have you arrested for menacing and carrying a loaded firearm."

"It's not loaded. I just wanted to scare the shit out of you."

"You did a good job. Now, Mr. Producer go back to your CDs and get ready for the show. Be thankful I didn't fire your ass. Don't ever pull anything like that again.

Get out."

"Mr. B.? Dancy Carter. Yes, it's a little hairy around here, sir. People pointing fingers and pointing guns, too.

"I'm okay. Things have settled down. DC is back in control.

"You're right about that. One down and one to go.

My regards to Mrs. B."

"Mr. Carter, this is Bob Woodstone of the Washington Post. We met at that fund raiser for the United Negro College Fund."

"Oh, yes. You're the famous investigative reporter who always carries a tape recorder. Remember you well."

"Thanks. That's my trademark. Never can tell when something important is said by an important person at an unimportant moment."

"What can I do for you, Mr. Woodstone?"

"Bob, Mr. Carter. Just Bob."

"Sure, and I'm just DC."

"I'm not sure. Just following up on a story about that society FBI agent killed in a car crash in Boston. I know he knew Jennifer Cabot at your station, but just learned that you knew him too. In fact, met with him a short time ago in Washington. Anything I should know about him, or why you met?"

"Hey, Bob, you really have good sources. That was a terrible tragedy. I asked a mutual friend to introduce me to Brian Dobbs because I had a problem that I thought he might help with."

"What kind of problem could Mr. Washington be having that would require the services of an FBI agent, an agent who worked out of Boston? Is there a story there?"

"I don't think so. The problem was of a personal nature."

"I didn't know that the Bureau was in the couch business, DC?"

"It wasn't personal like that. Someone was harassing me at home and on the air about my stances on various political issues. To add fat to the fire he was using a false name to gain access to me. He accused me of some egregious things. Did the same with associates and friends about me."

"Why the FBI and not the Washington P.D.?"

"Well it gets a little complicated. The person said he was a Professor of Political Science at Boston College. It just didn't smell right, so I asked some friends up there to check him out. Turns out there was no such professor at Boston College or any other in the area. A friend suggested I contact Mr. Dobbs, since he was headquartered in Boston. I asked him to check Bureau files for someone with that M.O., living in his area. I wasn't sure whether the intimidation or use of the phones to harass me were in violation of some Federal statute. Mr. Dobbs wasn't sure either, but said he would look into it. I didn't hear from him again."

"Did you follow it up?"

"Didn't need to, because the phone calls ceased. I felt it was some kind of a prank and was going to call Agent Dobbs to call off the hunt.

One question, Bob? Why is a nationally known reporter interested in something so obviously local?"

"It's the coincidence factor. Local events sometimes turn into national stories. Watergate for one: A third rate burglary brought down a sitting President."

"Are you suggesting that this incident has national implications of that magnitude?"

"Who knows, DC. An FBI agent mysteriously crashed into a wall a few miles from his home; that same agent has a meeting with a high-profile celebrity Dancy Carter, in Washington, about harassing phone calls and other intimidation by an unknown person using a false identity. Questions about a right wing group."

"What's the connection, Bob, coincidence or conspiracy?"

"Old snoop dog smells something. What, I don't know. Yet."

"Are you suggesting that the accident was not an accident?"

"Not at all."

"But you used the word mysteriously. That sort of moves it out of the ordinary accident category, to something more ominous."

"Just a reporter's habit, DC. Keeps my juices flowing. Keeps me snooping around."

"I guess that's why you break big stories that win Pulitzers."

"Can we go back to that phantom caller, DC? What else did he have to say?"

"Well, as I said, he asked about a secret right wing group in Washington. From the way he asked the question, my sense was he thought I knew them. Or worse yet, involved with them."

"Did you?"

"I didn't have a clue. There must be any number of groups around, especially in D.C. He never gave me a name."

"Ten minutes to air time, Mr. Carter," said his secretary over the intercom.

"Excuse me, Bob, have to go now. My audience is waiting. Nice talking to you. Hope you're wrong about Dobbs' accident."

"Thanks for the telephone time, DC. Go to it. You have a great show. Great music. Great stories. I listen often, even if I'm in the middle of writing a story. Sort of use your show as background. Do you take requests?"

"From my regular listeners, yes. From investigative journalists who are part-time listeners, maybe."

"This part-time listener would like to hear 'Miss New Orleans' by Satchmo. How about it?"

"You're in luck today, Bob. Got a Louis segment in the second hour. I'll add it to the list."

"See you at the next fund raiser, DC."

"Yeah, just bring your checkbook as well as your tape recorder."

"You're shameless, Mr. Carter."

The Boston Coroner's official report on Brian Dobbs' death was released, and the findings indicated he died from massive head injuries and a broken neck. His blood alcohol level was 0.18, more than twice the legal limit. Death was accidental. No foul play was involved. A tox screen for drugs would take a few more weeks to determine if that was a cause as well.

Dobbs' wife, Linda, was not convinced. She told his Bureau superiors and the police investigators that her husband hadn't taken a drink in over a year. He was a recovering alcoholic who attended AA meetings regularly.

The police told her the case was out of their hands since the Death Certificate from the M.E. declared it was an accident caused by drinking. And unless she had specific evidence to the contrary, the case was closed. There was a ray of hope, however, that if evidence surfaced that her husband was murdered, the case would be reopened. There was no statute of limitations on murder.

When the follow-up story of Brian Dobbs' accidental death appeared on the back pages of the Washington Post, Jennifer Cabot buzzed Dancy Carter. He didn't respond. She called three more times that morning and still no response. She rushed to the studio area a half hour before air time and found Carter at the console jotting down some notes. He never looked up.

"Dancy, you haven't answered any of my calls. Do I have to eat humble pie again?"

"You can eat what you want, just not at my table."

"The paper said it was an accident."

"Yes, I got that out of it, too."

"I want to apologize for accusing you of causing Brian's death. My emotions got the best of me, but I was way out of line accusing you without real proof."

"Not accepted, Miss Cabot. I guess needing proof wasn't taught in Harvard. You are a spoiled, social snob who speaks before thinking. You have done everything to destroy my trust in you, from lying to me about your involvement, romantic involvement, with Dobbs. Then incomprehensibly revealing AFTRA to him. And finally for making an irrational accusation tinged with uncalled for hate. No dear lady your apology is not accepted."

"Dancy, try and understand. I accused you because you said he had to be eliminated. I assumed you had something to do with it."

"Right on. If wishing had something to do with it, I'm guilty as hell. I wanted him dead, but only wished it to be. AFTRA is not some fun-for-the-rich-plaything. It's a cause. A cause I wholeheartedly believe in. I wholeheartedly abhor violence. Dobbs was a threat and it had to be stopped or AFTRA would be dead in the water. He was stopped, alright, by a concrete wall. Not by me."

"Can we have what we once had, DC?"

"I don't see how. I can't trust you and with what's at stake, trust is an absolute necessity."

"What can I do to get back your trust? Contribute more money? Swear to keep my lips sealed about AFTRA? What?"

"I know that's part of your upbringing, Jennifer, but you can't always buy your way out of a situation. Go back to Boston. Your kind is there. Parties, society, the Cabot legacy. That's your element. Please stay out of mine."

"Don't think you can brush me off so easily, Dancy Carter. We had a good thing going. I still love you, no matter what you think. Remember, however, that a woman scorned might not be responsible for her actions."

"That sounds like a threat. Just keep in mind the image of Brian Dobbs' car ramming into the concrete wall."

"Now that sounds like a real threat. Or is it an admission of some kind?"

"Hardly. Only a reminder that strange things happen if your hormones get mixed up with your intellect. It's almost air time, Miss Cabot. Gotta go to work. I suggest you go back to your office and monitor the show. Listen carefully. I guarantee to give you and the FCC something to shake up that bureaucracy in my first segment."

"Mr. Carter, Dancy, or rather DC, this is Carolyn Beaufort Cabot."

"Hello Carolyn Beaufort Cabot. Let me take a wild guess. You are Jennifer's mother."

"No jokes, DC. You know damn well who I am. My $200,000 checks to your precious AFTRA is the proof."

"Of course."

"Let's be serious, if we can?"

"Now where have I heard that before?"

"No sarcasm either. Serious, serious, DC."

"Serious it shall be, Mrs. Cabot. What do I owe the honor of this call?"

"A number of issues. But first some parental business. My daughter cried telling me that you've written her out of your life. Is that true?"

"Cried? I didn't think anything could make her cry."

"Serious, DC?"

"Yes, it's true."

"I thought you loved her. I know she loves you."

"I thought I did, too, but it's difficult to love someone you can't trust. And your daughter can't be trusted. AFTRA is not some society function that you go around inviting strangers to attend. It is a cause concerned Americans commit to knowing full well that being exposed can be deleterious to one's standing in the community. Worst case scenario: incarceration in a not-so-friendly Federal Prison Facility.

Your daughter committed the cardinal sin by violating the confidentiality of AFTRA. And to an agent of the FBI, no less. The person who arrests people who perpetrate crimes against the government, and helps fill up those not-so-friendly Federal Prison Facilities.

You see Mrs. Cabot, I have a real problem concerning that FBI agent. I know he's dead, but the information Jennifer gave him probably lives somewhere in his case file. That puts all of us in jeopardy because of her loose lips. She can't be trusted. Pure and simple."

"Did you have Dobbs eliminated, DC?"

"I answered that question for your daughter and others. It's insulting, not to mention laughable. I'm a commoner music man, not a hit man. According to the coroner he died driving too fast, with too much alcohol in him, into a concrete wall. And for the record, I don't have to defend myself to the Cabots, the Lodges, or the Schwartzes."

"I don't know the Schwartzes, DC, but aren't you getting a bit testy?"

"Sorry if you feel that, Mrs. Cabot. I'm just sick and tired about being asked the same nonsensical question."

"Okay, DC, I'm her mother, not her keeper. She's been an independent cuss for years. Hasn't listened to me from the day she was born. I wouldn't begin to try and influence her decisions about who she dates, who she marries."

"Come, come. Now you're not being truthful, Mrs. Cabot. You approved Brian Dobbs as marriage material for Jennifer because of his social pedigree. Dancy Carter was a commoner to be right for her. True?"

"Yes, it's true, but not for that reason. I wanted Dobbs to get off your case. Only that. If I could buy him off, he no longer would be a threat to AFTRA or you. I used Jennifer, unashamedly, to do that. That's the God's honest truth. I believe in AFTRA. I had to stop Dobbs, and if it meant putting my daughter in his bed, so be it. God only knows how many beds she's been in and out of since she was sixteen."

"That's not very motherly."

"I was counting on Jennifer to do what she usually did. The course she often took. That the flame would burn out and she would be on to her next victim. However, AFTRA was the only thing on my radar screen, not my daughter's love life."

"Now, now Mrs. Cabot, you know that's not true either."

"You're right, DC. You caught me in a little white lie."

"Again. That's two, dear lady. Three strikes and I'm out of here."

"Alright, down to business. I really called to talk about AFTRA. It's been two years now and I guess there's millions of dollars in the kitty. What's being done with the money."

"Progress, lots of it."

"Not that I can see, DC. I want evidence that White America is Right America is becoming a reality."

"We're working with deliberate speed, Mrs. Cabot. Bills have been tabled in Congress. Our people are entrenched in government agencies, and our friends in Congress are sponsoring legislation that will make our cause a reality."

"That sounds slow to me. It's my money and I want to be part of the process."

"Your money is working for you, Carolyn, and we don't need you working for your money. Satisfied?"

"Hardly, but I guess I have no other choice. It's clear as mud, and I think that's the way you want it to be."

"Watch the papers, dear lady. You'll see the results."

"It seems that's all I'm going to get, so back to my daughter. Give her another chance, DC. She's overwhelmed with guilt about selling you out. She loves you and wants you in her life, even though that would be a bitter pill for me to swallow. Boston society will crucify me."

"You can handle that. You're tough. You're a Cabot."

"Maybe. Crucified or not, a mother is still a mother and what Jennifer wants I want. Social stains or not. Do you want me to beg?"

"I would never ask that of you. I just need time. Jennifer should have known better. She's spoiled rotten."

"To say the least, DC."

"I have to consider whether another romantic dalliance will produce another bout of loose lips. You'll know when she knows. By the way, being a mother is not such a bad thing."

"Zack, come on in and wipe that sheepish look off your face. What's up?"

"DC, I guess it's my turn to apologize."

"How do you know it's your turn?"

"Spoke to Miss Cabot and she said she offered up an apology. I hope I have better acceptance luck than she did?"

"Depends on what you say."

"I waited till the show was over to collect my thoughts."

"Are they collected?"

"Come on, DC. I'm serious, very serious."

"What the hell is this serious disease? There must be a serious germ in the air. Everybody seems to have caught it lately. Go ahead be serious."

"DC, I don't think you had anything to do with Brian Dobbs' murder."

"Accident, Zack. Accident."

"Yeah, accident. I'm sure that's what you want everyone to believe. Was it really an accident?"

"What, no gun this time, Mr. Zoltowski? Wasn't this to be apology time?"

"God, I want to believe you, DC. I prayed that you had nothing to do with Brian's death. My gut instinct tells me there's more here than meets the eye. And you know much, much more. I have no proof, and the M.E.'s report calls it an accident. So I apologize."

"That's a non-apology. Hard to believe you think it is one. And the but is overwhelmingly negative."

"This is not coming out the way I rehearsed it."

"Rehearsed it? You had to rehearse a simple apology? What the hell does that mean?"

"The apology is real for accusing you of murder, the but is about AFTRA."

"AFTRA? What does the American Federation of Television and Radio Artists have to do with this?"

"No jokes, DC. I'm talking about your secret right wing group that's out to change the color of America. What I'm saying will cost me my job,. So before I'm fired, here's my letter of resignation."

"Zack, Zack! If I didn't fire you when you foolishly pointed a gun at my head, do you think the gibberish you're mouthing now would make me pull the rug out from under your job? A job you really need and want."

"I don't know what to think. It's all confusing."

"I suggest you get real. Stop living in some fantasy world of conspiracy. Dobbs' world."

"He may be dead, DC, but it's like he spoke from the grave or knew he could die when he told me about

AFTRA...and you. I was reluctant to believe him, but he made a strong case."

"Strong? It was all pie in the sky."

"Not to me. Right or wrong, I bought in and decided to smoke you out and expose a radical group."

"That stuff you're smoking must be very powerful, friend. Forget about what he told you, how he sold you. Where's the proof, I mean documented proof about such a group, much less it even exists?"

"Only his word, DC. An FBI agent's word."

"Yeah, an agent with a checkered past concerning you. No matter. Without any proof, why would anyone believe a word you say? It's your word, a disgruntled employee's word, against the word of the champion of liberal causes."

"You're right. That's why I'm quitting. It would be very hard working with you every day, pretending everything was normal. More likely abnormal, and possibly being the guy who puts you in jail."

"Now that's mighty white of you Zoltowski. Jail is certainly not an appealing prospect."

"Accept my resignation, DC. Make it easy on both of us."

"No, my apologetic friend, it's all easy and irrelevant. I have nothing to hide. Nothing to watch out what I say. Nothing that remotely links me with any radical group. Nothing that would put me in jail. Nothing. Don't quit on my part."

"Why can't I just believe you, DC?"

"Believe me. This whole thing was a figment of Dobbs' imagination. If he could have made a case for its existence, for my involvement, and if he had probable cause, subpoenas would have been issued to search my studio, my apartment, my bank records. Anything and everything."

"He said he was putting a case together, but was biding his time. Said he had a good reason."

"There's a good reason why he didn't. There is no right-wing group called AFTRA on record anywhere. Not in the D.C.'s County Clerk's office…the phone book…any bank…any listing in any office building. You'd have to exhume Dobb's body to see if he has it imprinted on his brain."

"Don't do that, DC. Don't patronize me. Dobbs believed he was onto something and I believed him."

"Why?"

"Call it agent-agent instinct."

"Ok, Zoltowski. The fencing is over. Believe what you want. Investigate till the cows come home. You'll find nothing. Right now, however, I need you on my show, so your job is safe. I have no hard feelings even with your half-assed apology. Let's get the show on the road. Are the Goodman CDs ready?"

"Yes. Any intro?"

"Open with the eight minute version of **'SING, SING, SING.'** No intro."

* * *

The next morning about 12 noon, Carter walked down the hall to Jennifer Cabot's office. Her back was turned away from the door and she was on the phone. Not willing to wait, Carter walked around her desk and gave her the radio cut-off sign, a hand across the neck. She quickly hung up.

"Miss Cabot, I have a personnel problem. Zoltowski hasn't come in for our usual pre-production meeting. He's an hour and a half late. I checked his log and all today's CDs are in place. Get me an engineer."

"What happened to him? Did he call? Aren't you concerned?"

"Don't know. Not a word. Not concerned."

"Do you think he's had some kind of 'ACCIDENT'?"

"There seems to be some kind of accusation in that question. Are you implying a Brian Dobbs kind of accident?

Your silence speaks volumes, Miss Cabot. However, I didn't come here to rehash accidents. I have a show to do, so get an engineer into the studio pronto...or sooner. Can you do that little thing?"

Carter turned and left without waiting for her response. If he did, he would have seen a shaken look on her face and a wide open mouth.

Ten minutes before 'DC ON THE AIR' was going on the air, a harried Zack Zoltowski rushed into the studio breathing heavily, as if he had been running. Blood was dripping down the right side of his face, a nasty gash over his right eye.

"Sorry I'm late, DC, but I was rear-ended on the Beltway and hit my head on the steering wheel. My old car doesn't have air bags."

"Are you all right?"

"Just a little woozy, but the cobwebs are starting to disappear. I know the CDs are in place, do you want to go over the rundown?"

"No. Jim Brant is filling in for you. Take the rest of the day, and get that gash taken care of at the infirmary."

"I'm ok, DC. Really ok. Tell Jim I'll take over. Just need a strong cup of coffee to calm me down."

"Coffee doesn't do that. Maybe a stiff drink. Oh, I forgot you don't drink anymore. Sorry. No matter, I'm ordering you to take the day off."

"Come on, DC, don't baby me. I want to work. All the Goodman CDs are racked up and ready to go. I know you wanted to open with SING, SING, SING, but I'd like to save that for later in the show. I suggest opening with his theme song, 'LET'S DANCE.' Is that ok with you?"

"Fine, fine, but I wish you would take the day off. Cabot had that accusatory look in her eyes that maybe you had a Brian Dobbs kind of accident. That look was disturbing, so I'd rather have you take off today."

"Look or no look. I'm okay. Ok as in just fine."

"You win, Zoltowski. Put on the headphones, we're coming up on 1:00 PM. Cue me for the opening."

"Miss Cabot? This is Bob Woodstone of the Washington Post. I'm following up on a story we ran on the death of your friend, FBI Agent Brian Dobbs. If you're not too busy, may we talk a few minutes?"

"Well I'm not only busy, but a trifle upset over his death."

"Sorry about that. I can call at another time."

"No, sir. Let's do it now, although I'm not quite certain why you want to speak to me?"

"I don't know either, Miss Cabot, but my source tells me that Agent Dobbs was onto something big before his untimely death."

"All good and well, but what does that have to do with me?"

"Don't know yet, but you knew Dobbs rather intimately some time ago back in Boston, and Dancy Carter intimated that the two of you were more than telephone friends."

"You could say that. We were romantically involved way back when. So far back that it's just a blur now. We ran into each other in Washington, shortly before the accident."

"By design?"

"No, by accident. He was at the station meeting with Dancy Carter and his producer, a former friend of his. Mr. Carter had some kind of harassment issue with a call-in that he thought the FBI, Dobbs, could help with."

"Why the FBI?"

"Don't know."

"Would that producer be Zack Zoltowski?"

"Yes, Zack. Mr. Woodstone, I'm puzzled. Why are we discussing Brian Dobbs' meeting with Dancy Carter? All I know is that they met about harassment. Zack arranged the meeting."

"I'm puzzled too, Miss Cabot, especially since my source at the Bureau says they don't believe Dobbs' death was an accident. They are investigating that as we speak. Also the case file is still open on what Dobbs was investigating."

"Carter's harassment issue?"

"Something more. Much more sinister."

"I have no idea what Dobbs was investigating. And the Bureau must know that the Coroner's office ruled his death accidental. Your paper printed the findings, Mr. Woodstone."

"True, but the Bureau is saying something else. Not an accident, but murder."

"Murder? That's insane. Why would someone go to such an elaborate scheme to make a murder look like an accident?"

"Good question. Do you have an answer?"

"I repeat, Mr. Woodstone, the murder idea is insane."

"When you saw Agent Dobbs did he hint at anything Dancy Carter said that could be considered suspicious?"

"Are you listening carefully, Mr. Woodstone? I told you I knew why Carter was meeting with Dobbs. Dobbs never mentioned a thing about their meeting."

"My source says that Dobbs had information, confidential source information, that Dancy Carter was involved with a radical right-wing group."

"You've got to be kidding? Dancy Carter? No way. The man is involved with every liberal organization in Washington. You name it, he's right in the middle of it. Raising money, marching in some protest. DC is the most dedicated liberal in D.C."

"Oh, so I guess there's no story there?"

"My guess is that your guess is right."

"You've given me a great deal of time, Miss Cabot. I appreciate that, especially knowing you're upset about something. Thanks. If I may, I have just one more question."

"And that is, sir."

"You admitted an affair with Agent Dobbs, have you been seeing Dancy Carter 'socially'?"

"No comment, sir. And don't read anything positive into that."

"Fair enough. Not prying, just trying to tie up some loose ends. Thanks again for your valuable time."

"Mr. Zoltowski? Hi, this is Bob Woodstone of the Washington Post."

"*The* Bob Woodstone? What do I owe the honor?"

"First let me apologize for calling you at home, but they told me at the station that you left for the day after the show. Something about an accident."

"Oh, that accident...I thought you were talking about...I was rear ended on the Beltway. But you didn't call me at this time of night to commiserate with me about a fender-bender. Now did you? A minor fender-bender at that."

"No sir. I called to talk to you about a major accident that took the life of your FBI friend, Brian Dobbs."

"That was sad, very sad. A tragic accident. Is there a reason for your interest in an accident? You have a major reputation as an investigative reporter on national issues. Why the interest in a local accident?"

"I really didn't until a source at the Bureau said it wasn't an accident. That Dobbs was murdered. He also said that you were working with him investigating some high profile media celebrity who was fronting a right wing group."

"Murder? I hadn't heard that. For the record, I wasn't working with him. Not exactly. When I was an agent, years ago, Dobbs and I were partnered up. He asked me, for old times' sake, to keep an eye on some of the right wing groups operating in Washington."

"Was Dancy Carter someone to keep an eye on?"

"Not him directly, but any of the political personalities that Carter interviewed on 'DC ON THE AIR.' Dobbs had what I considered a hare-brain theory that a radio personality who interviewed political people might elicit information about these right wing groups. He also thought I might learn some tidbits during the pre-show interview. I felt it was just a long shot, but being a friend I agreed to help."

"So evidently he thought that Dancy Carter might be involved with that kind of group?"

"I didn't say that, Mr. Woodstone. As I said, maybe some information could be gleaned from the interviews. He never said he suspected Carter was involved."

"Did you learn anything from the interviews?"

"Not anything that I heard directly."

"Do you think Carter did?"

"You'd have to ask him. Not to change the subject, Mr. Woodstone, but why would you believe the Bureau saying Dobbs was murdered, when the M.E. reported it was an accident?"

"You were at the Bureau, Mr. Zoltowski. You know how they think. Why do you think they believe he was murdered?"

"I don't think anything, sir. All I know is what I read, and it spells accident in capital letters."

"Come on. Can you think of any reason the Bureau would go out on a limb like that? Especially to a reporter?"

"That's an easy one, sir. Especially to a reporter. The Bureau is paranoid when an agent dies under less than on-duty circumstances. The first thing they see is some sort of conspiracy. It's built into the system. Dobbs probably convinced his supervisor he was onto something big. His boss in turn would put two and two together and come up with murder. And leaking it to a top investigative reporter was a way to keep the idea alive. Dobbs was a good agent who had a fertile imagination."

"Do you think he made up this right wing group?"

"Could be. In any case it was self-serving. Dobbs was in danger of being drummed out of the Bureau for drinking and some other things. My feeling is that he invented that right wing group and hinted that a Dancy Carter-like personality was involved to get me interested, and to convince the top brass that he was onto something. Something big in Washington. It would be a feather in his cap to expose such a group and save his job. Save his career."

"It's odd, Zack, that you felt it was a contrived story, yet you agreed to work with him?"

"Work with him? Not really. Help? Yeah. A friend is a friend is a friend, Mr. Woodstone. Especially a former partner. Loyalty is what they preach and teach at the Bureau. If I could help save his job, I would try, harebrained idea or not."

"Weren't you jeopardizing your friendship and your job by spying on your boss?"

"Spying? I wasn't spying, Mr. Woodstone. I was just listening to what others might say to him. Nothing more. I told Dobbs flat out that he was off on a wild goose chase, but would go along to prove he was chasing a shadow."

"Another source, told me you offered to resign because you believed that Dobbs was murdered. And somehow Carter was involved. How does that square with what you've said?"

"Your source was only half right. I wanted to quit because my raise never came through. I was pissed off and made that threat. Only half-heartedly, I might add. It had nothing to do with my thinking that Dancy Carter was involved."

"So what happened?"

"Carter got me the raise."

"No right wing group with Carter into it up to his armpits?"

"I never said that, Mr. Woodstone. You're a good writer, but don't put words in my mouth. If DC was ever involved he would have to clone himself. He's into so many liberal causes day and night that make it impossible for him to find the time to be part of a right wing group. Without somebody finding out. Just no way."

"Guess the Bureau is chasing ghosts, too, eh Zack?"
"Iguess. Probably protecting their turf, Mr. Woodstone."

"Thanks for your time, Zack. Hope your cut heals quickly. Try to stay away from accidents. Oh, just one more thing. Do you know if Carter is having an affair with Miss Cabot?"

"Not to my knowledge, but if I did know, I wouldn't tell you anyway. Good night, sir."

"Thanks again, Zack. You've been very helpful."

"Good, good day D.C. And what a day it is. A balmy, almost spring-like 60 degree day with the sun splashing all over the nation's capitol. Oh, yes, this is your Music Man DC, Dancy Carter with 'DC ON THE AIR' on WTOP 1500 on your AM dial—your favorite music listening post from 1-3 PM, Monday thru Friday. Ah, but you know that.

To celebrate this glorious weather, I've changed the program and will give you two hours of vocals and instrumentals about the weather. Sunny songs, rainy songs, stormy songs.

And that's my cryptic lead-in to some of Tin-Pan Alleys' great songs by America's great composers and lyricists, sung by song stylists you love and bands you do your dancing to. To get your juices flowing, here's a sample of what DC will be playing for you. 'SPRING WILL BE A LITTLE LATE THIS YEAR' by the incomparable Ella Fitzgerald, 'INDIAN SUMMER,' the sultry version by Francis Albert Sinatra, 'STORMY WEATHER,' by the fiery, beautiful, belle of the south, Lena Horne, and 'WE'RE HAVING A HEAT WAVE,' by the lady with the big pipes who never needed a microphone, Ethel Merman. And much, much more.

So sit back folks, think about the lovely weather outside while you enjoy our parade of weather songs on the station where the sun always shines, and music reigns. That's R-E-I-G-N-S. It's a pun folks. The DC funny for today.

Now keep it right here on WTOP 1500 on your AM dial with 'DC ON THE AIR' right up until 3 PM.

Ok Mr. Producer hit the play button and let Miss Judy Garland brighten your day with her timeless version of 'SOMEWHERE OVER THE RAINBOW,' the Harold Arlen classic from the Wizard of Oz."

"Zack, did you find Nat Cole's CD with 'AUTMN LEAVES?' Want to start the second hour with that."

"Got it in my hot little hands, DC. By the way, got a call from Bob Woodstone of the Washington Post."

"*The* Bob Woodstone? The Pulitzer Prize Bob Woodstone?"

"One and the same, DC."

"He's an investigative reporter, Zack. What was he investigating about you?"

"Not me. He only wanted background info on Brian Dobbs."

"Why you?"

"Don't know, but he knew that we were partners years ago at the Bureau and that we had met recently."

"That's a lot of investigating for a rather insignificant connection, don't you think?"

"I really don't know what to think. He said a source at the Bureau told him that Dobbs' death was not an accident. Surprised me. Then he asked for my opinion."

"About whether it was an accident?"

"No, if the source was giving it to him straight. I told him the Bureau always suspects foul play anytime they lose an agent to an accident, heart attack or the gout. That was it. He thanked me and hung up."

"Did any agent ever die from the gout, Zack?"

"Never heard of one, but he caught me by surprise and gout seemed like a serious disease.

Thirty seconds to air, DC. Do you want a commercial break or Lena Horne?"

"Lena, Zacko. The killer gout. Now that's funny."

***

"DC! Bob Woodstone again. Forgive me for calling you at home, but I've been in Boston all day. We need to talk. Can we?"

"Yeah, sure, Bob. You've been calling everyone else, why not me? How did you ever get my private number?"

"I never reveal my sources, DC."

"Touché, Robert. I respect that right. So what's so urgent that you had to call in a favor to call me at home?"

"Dobbs."

"The man is dead, Bob, can't you let him rest in peace? And what's so compelling that a reporter of national stature is stirring up the bones of someone who died in an accident?"

"Unanswered questions of how he died."

"Unanswered? The M.E. answered that Mr. Reporter. I'm sure you've read his report?"

"Over and over. That's why I decided to meet with him face to face in Boston. He was puzzled that Dobbs' blood alcohol level was 0.18."

"Puzzled? When someone drinks more than he should, gets behind the wheel of a car and drives into a concrete wall, 0.18 doesn't seem to be puzzling. I think I read somewhere that drinking and driving don't mix. Usually causes an accident where someone dies."

"Logical, DC. But what was puzzling was that Dobbs was a recovering alcoholic and hadn't had a drink in some time."

"Not puzzling to me. What's so unusual about a former drunk falling off the wagon? Besides that, why are we having this discussion about Dobbs' drinking habits? I barely knew the man, much less any of his habits."

"You're absolutely right, yet something doesn't add up, Mr. Carter."

"Well, now we're into the real reason for this call if you're calling me Mr. Carter."

"Sorry about that, DC. Just out of habit."

"You want to talk, *Bob*? Well, my sense is that you want me to listen. Shoot."

"It goes like this: Jennifer Cabot and Brian Dobbs were lovers in Boston years ago. They renewed their affair recently."

"Is that for sure, Bob?"

"As far as I can determine."

"Go on."

"Dobbs and Zoltowski are old friends, FBI agents joined at the hip as partners ten years ago. The question is why did Dobbs contact him after no contact for years?"

"I'm guessing, Bob, but maybe he felt guilty about his role in Zack's termination and wanted to clear the air."

"Not even close. He had another agenda, that is to convince Zolo (his real name) that a right wing group led by a well-known DJ existed in Washington. He asked for his help to unmask this guy."

"Did Zack give it to him?"

"More than that. My source tells me he reupped as a part-time agent. What's more the appointment was pre-approved by the Director."

"Reupped? He has a job here."

"Dobbs' then under an assumed name, Professor Doyle, contacted the celebrity DJ to push his button about the secret group. Sound familiar so far?"

"I think I heard it before."

"The DJ suspected that Dobbs and Doyle were one and the same. Yet asked Zack to arrange a meeting with Dobbs to investigate Doyle to determine if any Federal statute was broken. Strange, to say the least."

"Not for me, Bob."

"Dobbs agreed to see if his 'alter ego' had committed a Federal offense. In other words, he would be investigating himself. Really strange, agree?"

"No. I wanted to trick him into admitting he was Doyle. And he did."

"Then Mr. Dobbs died under stranger circumstances before he could respond to the DJ's request."

"Stranger circumstances, Bob? The man died in an automobile accident, officially recorded as an accident on a Death Certificate by the Boston M.E. Not some clerk in the morgue."

"That's on the record, DC. Off the record the Bureau says murder."

"I thought they said it was gout."

"Gout? I don't understand."

"It's an inside joke, Bob. Are you finished talking? If so please tell me what you're getting to. No more cat and mouse games."

"Fair enough, DC. The DJ I am patently avoiding to identify is you."

"No kidding! I never would have guessed it."

"Well I had my reasons."

"Good ones I'm sure. For the record, everything you've spelled out is exactly what took place. So what? I've heard all of this time and time again from friends as well as enemies. So what? Is there a point?"

"Is there a right wing secret group in Washington D.C., DC?"

"Absolutely. Some I've heard of and others I haven't."

"Is there one headed by you? Before answering, it's no crime to be part of a right or left wing political group. You can bay at the moon as long as you don't commit a crime."

"Thank you, Mr. Pulitzer Prize, for your lawyer's opinion on the laws governing crimeless political activity."

"Forgive me for patronizing you, DC."

"Look, Bob, wherever you're going with your question, you're going in the wrong direction. Look for another DJ, you've got the wrong one in me."

"We're on the record, right DC?"

"Turn up the volume on your tape recorder, Bob, because on or off the record I haven't a clue as to what you're implying."

"I'm not recording this, DC."

"Don't care. Dobbs died crashing into a concrete wall while driving drunk. I didn't serve him any drinks, and I didn't have my hands on the wheel. It was an accident. An accident. The police report said so and the M.E. put it on paper for everyone to see."

"DC, maybe everything was contrived by a desperate agent, but there are too many coincidences for me to ignore. It's my job to investigate."

"Investigate till you're blue in the face, but unless you find irrefutable evidence that I'm involved, that it was foul play, back off about me."

"Why the hell did Dobbs single you out?"

"He wanted to nail somebody, anybody to save his career, so he created from whole cloth a scenario about a DJ heading up a radical right wing group. I happened to be the liberal DJ with the most celebrity. That was juicy. I was fair game."

"I still have to look into it, DC."

"Look all you want, sir, but you won't find a single fingerprint of mine in any of this."

"Believe me, DC, I want to believe you."

"Thanks for your vote of confidence. Sorry if I seem rude, but I have a dinner date. I have to go now."

"Thanks for your time, DC. Enjoy dinner."

"Mr. Dancy Carter? This is Mr. B. There are events happening that are interfering with a good night's sleep. We need to talk, Mr. Carter."

Dancy was puzzled by the formal Dancy Carter and Mr. Carter instead of the usual friendly, hi DC how-are-you greeting. Not good, he thought. He decided to be very upbeat.

"Mr. B! Glad you called. You must have been reading my mind. I was just about to call you and fill you in on a number of things. Some disturbing enough to be addressed immediately."

"I didn't read your mind, Carter, but make it quick before I tell you what's on my mind."

"Bob Woodstone of the Washington Post has been sniffing around about the Dobbs' incident. It seems to be at the top of his investigative project list."

"I know that. Get on with it."

"I'm not actually sure why, but he has put a full court press on Jennifer Cabot, Zack Zoltowski, the FBI, the M.E. and me. Questions. Questions. Subtle accusations."

"Hurry up."

"His source at the Bureau says that Dobbs was murdered. Not a problem, since they never accept an accidental death of an agent, especially a drunken accident. Murder is more to their liking. It's an image thing."

"So what is the problem?"

"Woodstone hinting that Dobbs' case file makes a reference to the existence of AFTRA...not in name but in concept. A crack investigative reporter like Woodstone doesn't need more than a hint of a juicy conspiracy to go full bore on the story. That's a problem."

"I should imagine so. So?"

"He believes his source is credible and murder is more than just a maybe. When he adds a bunch of coincidences to what he thinks he knows, leads him to believe there's a real story here. It's only a matter of time before he figures it out. That's a real problem."

"Get to the point, dammit. Now."

"I think we should cut him off at the pass. Use your influence with the Post people to have them call off their attack dog. Or hopefully find out if he has any hard information that's hiding under his pillow. It's possible that he has nothing but bits of innuendo and Bureau paranoia to go on, and his Pulitzer Prize investigative inquisitiveness that's driving him."

"I don't need your advice on any of this, Carter."

"Sorry, Mr. B, I wasn't offering advice, just a suggestion."

"I don't need any suggestion either. Is there anything else? I'm just about at the end of my patience."

"One more problem, sir. Carolyn Cabot. She's a bit edgy about the bang she's getting for her buck. Wants to see more results more quickly. And definitely wants to be more involved."

"She's being handled."

"Good. So to sum it all up in one sentence: Woodstone smells smoke, but he can't locate the fire. Yet."

"Are you through now, Mr. Carter?"

"Yes. Sorry if I was rather wordy, but I wanted you to get a clear picture of what was happening."

"I got the picture. In fact, I knew everything there was to know before you said it. I was briefed in full. I have a different problem to address. And it's not Woodstone, not Cabot, not the FBI, not anyone. It's you."

"Me? What about me?"

"You are too visible. Your show, your opinions, your attempts to joke your way out of any involvement in the Dobbs' incident is allowing the light to shine too brightly on you."

"I'm DC, Mr. B. The light is always on me."

"I don't like that kind of illumination. Don't need it either. I want you to back off."

"Back off to where?"

"Be far less political on the show. Be more involved with all your causes, and less with controversy."

"That's what my audience tunes in for."

"Well, as of now, I'm tuning you out. No more interviews with Woodstone. No more dinners with Jennifer Cabot. Get back with your black girl. Play your music and nothing but your music."

"That's a lot of don'ts. Seems that my involvement with AFTRA has gone from major player to minor role."

"Excellent conclusion, Mr. Carter."

"Why?"

"You are a liability to us, and we can't afford any liabilities. Too many fingers pointed at you, and that is not healthy for us. From now on, John Cabot will be in charge in Washington. In truth, I don't want you to do anything at all. Is that clear? And absolutely no more goodbyes to Mrs. B at show's end. Is that clear?"

"What the hell did I do to deserve being sent to the back of the bus, Mr. B?"

"Instead of being the leader, you've become a lightning rod attracting the wrong kind of attention. Attracting the attention of a Bob Woodstone. That's courting trouble. He's rapidly connecting the dots about your involvement with Dobbs, and eventually will draw a straight line to AFTRA and me."

"I've given too much to the cause to be treated like this, Mr. B. I don't deserve it. What's more, I won't stand for it. I'm DC."

"Yes you will, Mr. Carter. The alternative might not be in your best interest."

"Is that a threat?"

"I don't threaten. Just reality. I appreciate what you've done, but for now you'll take orders, and take a back seat. Maintain a low profile."

"How do I do that, sir? I am high profile."

"Good. Be the DC that every liberal thinks the world of. Be the DC that your audience adores. Do all that and you deflect attention from you, and AFTRA is not in the eye of the storm. You opened a Pandora's Box with the Doyle/Dobbs issue. That put bad things in motion."

"I was only testing the water, to see if Doyle was real. I never thought it would lead to Dobbs or the FBI."

"That's what I mean. You were over your head in 8 feet of water. Not good if you can't swim. One other thing, Mr. Carter. Do not call me again. If I want you for anything I'll contact you. Stay out of the bright lights."

I'm in the bright lights with 'DC ON THE AIR.' How do I avoid that?"

"No problem there. That's the good light. Make it shine brighter."

"I'm confused by the lights...Mr. B. Are you there?"

The phone line went dead.

When he slammed the phone back on its cradle, Carter's anger exploded into a stream of obscenities.

"That sanctimonious son-of-a-bitch," he roared. "He can't do that to me after all I've done for him. I'm Dancy Carter, the DC of D.C. I can put his ass in a sling in a minute. That bastard can't put me out to pasture so easily. I have the goods on him, big time. Enough to put him in a place without windows. Where his pin-stripe suit will be exchanged for a different kind of pin-striped suit."

He poured himself a double shot of Jack Daniels and sat back in his lounge chair. He replayed over and over the idea that Mr. B thought he was a liability. He could not believe he went from being a primary asset to a liability. As the alcohol started to take the edge off his anger, and his jangled emotions, he was reminded of the veiled threat that Mr. B tossed out in that controlling voice he used with great effect. It had a chilling effect. He wondered if Mr. B really meant he would become another Dobbs accident.

Carter poured himself another double shot of Jack Daniels. He quickly realized it had little or no effect in controlling the sense of fear that came over him. He started to shake all over. He was now at his wit's end. Frightened. Out in the cold. Alone. He knew he had to get out of that sinkhole called AFTRA. But how? Even with Jack Daniels dulling his senses, the idea struck him like a bolt of lightning. Get to the guy who was trying to get him. Bob Woodstone, that's the guy. That's how. The man was looking for a story, so I'll give him a story that has Pulitzer Prize 2 written all over it. He would be his "Deep Throat." Brilliant was all he could think of. That would be his way out. Bob Woodstone. He hoped his tape recorder was in good working condition.

Carter kicked off his shoes. His fear abated, but well aware that he was in for a firestorm. Bob Woodstone and being Washington's number one celebrity would put up a firewall to protect him. As his eyelids became heavy, he mumbled something about Mr. B having political power. Didn't compare with the people power DC had going for him. He drifted off into a whiskey initiated sound sleep with a huge smile on his face.

"Hello there folks in D.C. land. My watch says 1:00 PM. You know what that means. Time for your friendly music man, DC, Dancy Carter with two exciting hours of 'DC ON THE AIR' on WTOP, 1500 on your AM dial. Your number one station in our nation's capitol for great music. News on the half hour and weather. Ah but you know that.

The music you hear in the background is the blues. And that's my mood today. Woke up feeling a little blue. Don't know why because it rarely happens to DC. So I said to myself, self, the best prescription for putting the blues behind me is to play the best blues recording we could rustle up.

And that's exactly what we're going to do. For the next two hours it's the blues, blues, blues. No, that doesn't mean sad, mournful music. Not at all. Many of the songs you'll hear will be upbeat. Full of life. Some soulful, some sinful, but all blues. All shades of blue.

"We've racked up old favorites like 'BASIN STREET BLUES,' 'BLUES IN THE NIGHT,' 'KANSAS CITY BLUES,' ST LOUIS BLUES,' and lots more. Artists like Louis 'Satchmo' Armstrong, Count Basie and his favorite son, Joe Williams, Jimmy Rushing and the incomparable Bessie Smith. Yeah it might be a blue Monday, but when we're through you'll be feeling might good. And so will the DC man. Count on it.

So kick back, grab a cold one, your favorite carbonated beverage, that is, put your feet up on your foot-friendly hassock and keep it right here on WTOP, 1500 on your AM dial. It's 'DC ON THE AIR, and I'm DC, Dancy Carter. Blues be gone.

Mr. Producer raise the gain on that volume and let's fill the airwaves with Mr. Joe Williams and the Count with a stirring version of 'I'VE GOT A RIGHT TO SING THE BLUES'"

"How was that folks? Did you shoo the blues? I did for sure. Feeling better and with what else we have in store it's only going to get even better. So before the great Bessie Smith comes wailing into your living room, let's attend to a little business. Just one commercial to help pay some bills, and then we're back with our blues on parade festival."

***

"Good show boss man. Why so blue today?"
"I have no idea why I woke up feeling blue this morning. Think I had some bad dreams during the night."
"How come no goodbye to Mrs. B? Is she out of favor?"

"Forgot Zack. Caught up with the blues stuff and plain out forgot."

"How do you feel now?"

"Better, Zack. Happy as a lark."

"Ditto for me Dancy. Dobbs' death had me feeling kinda low, but when you hear the blues the way those great artists go at it, feeling low is turned into a high. Thanks, DC. You did it again. That's why you're the best. The king of music. May you reign forever."

"Thank you, Zack. At least until the next show."

"Bob Woodstone! This is—"

"I know. It's DC. Recognize those dulcet tones. What's up?"

"Need to talk. Can we meet someplace private?"

"How private?"

"Someplace dark and underground where nobody can see or hear what I have to say."

"Sounds mysterious, DC, but very intriguing. How about my garage at the Watergate? Level 3. Hardly anyone there. Not many cars. Make it 5:00 PM."

"Perfect. Just one request, Bob. No pad. No tape recorder. Just you and your memory. Agreed?"

"Really intriguing. Agreed."

"Satin doll? It's the DC man. How's my chocolate colored dream girl?"

"Not holding my breath waiting to hear from the vanilla man. I guess your dialing finger was hit with a bad case of arthritis?"

"Kinda busy. Interviews. Charities. It's not easy being a celebrity."

"Yeah, sure. Well Mr. Celebrity, you must want something from me. Am I close?"

"Sure do."

"Sorry, but if its action you want, uh, uh. This week is not good, it's that time of the month."

"Not that kind of action, doll. Just dinner and a few laughs for old times' sake. I miss the fun we used to have."

"No fun with that white chick?"

"No comment lady."

"Well, what do you have in mind? Or rather what time should I meet you at Dukes?"

"Still read me like an open book, doll face. Dukes it is, but I'll pick you up. We're going in style. Got a limo, a chauffeur, flowers and me. It's a special night."

"My, my Mr. Washington. That sounds like a perfect let's-be-friends night."

"8 PM, beautiful lady. Dress your best. I'll be wearing a tux."

On the third level of the Watergate garage, Bob Woodstone waited in the shadows for his intriguing meeting with Dancy Carter. Virtually the only light was the faint glow of his cigarette. He looked at his watch for the third time and it was past 5:00 PM. Carter was nowhere in sight. Woodstone was about to leave when Dancy Carter appeared out of the shadows without making a sound. His fedora was pulled down over his eyes and the collar of his Burberry pulled up covering almost half of his face.

"Dancy is that you? I can barely see your face."

"It's me."

"Why are you whispering? What's going on? And why are we meeting in the dark? Not to mention why all the spy-like clothing?"

"I have my reasons. First, Bob, what I'm about to tell you is not for attribution by me. When you write your story, in no way will it include or mention me, or even hint who I am. I'm your Deep Throat. Agreed?"

"If you didn't sound so serious, your get-up, meeting at Watergate, and your resurrecting Deep Throat, all this would be laughable. Especially Deep Throat. Notice, DC, I'm not laughing. I realize you're serious. Very serious. However, let me hear what you have to say before I agree to anything."

"Bob, I'm using Deep Throat to emphasize that my identity is never to be disclosed. I repeat never. In a story. To anyone at the Post. Or anywhere at any time. Agree or I walk."

"I'll try."

"Uh, uh. Not good enough Woodstone. These are the ground rules or there's no story."

"Alright. I agree, but it better be good, DC, or the rules will be broken."

"For now, I'm only going to give you one part, just the bare bones of this sordid story. You're going to use all your investigative skills to put the pieces in place."

"I'm listening, DC. Let's get on with it."

"For today, it's about Brian Dobbs. His death was no accident, he was murdered."

"I have that already, DC. I need proof."

"What he drank and why it made him crash is for you to find out. Proof? Here's a clue: check the M.E.'s report again. Speak to him again. Ask him to look carefully for something in the tox screen that he missed. It's definitely there."

"What else?"

"That's it for now. Once you find out he was murdered, everything else I tell you will make the story whole. When I want us to meet again, I'll leave word that a package will be delivered. We'll meet that day, right here at the same time."

"You're not kidding about that 'Deep Throat' thing, are you DC? When do you think that next time will be?"

When Woodstone looked up Carter was gone. He left as quietly as when he arrived.

"Dancy?"

Woodstone took the tape recorder out of his coat pocket and played back the entire conversation. "The tox screen. Interesting. Sorry about the tape recorder, DC, but my memory is not as good as it used to be."

When the elevator doors on the main level of the garage opened, Dancy Carter came face to face with Jennifer Cabot.

"DC is that you in that getup? You look like the spy that came in from out of the cold. What are you doing in the garage?"

"Hello, Miss Cabot. I was looking for a friend's apartment."

"He lives in the garage?"

"No, of course not. I must have pushed the wrong button."

"Yes, in the wrong elevator, too. Have you been drinking, DC?"

"No."

"Well you look terrible. Pale and somewhat out of it. Are you sick?"

"I'm not sick. Just tired. I have to go now."

"Wait. What were you doing here? Answer me."

"I can't."

"You can't or you won't."

"Both, Boston lady. Please don't press me any further. I don't want you to know anything about anything."

"Does the anything have to do with Brian Dobbs' death? Dancy, say something."

"There's nothing to say. Excuse me. I must go."

"Come up to my apartment and I'll fix you a drink and we can talk."

"Good night, Miss Cabot. See you at the shop."

She watched him walk away. His shoulders hunched. The body language of a frightened man. Not DC. He needed help.

"Miss Cabot. Good evening."

"Mr. Woodstone? I didn't know you lived at Watergate?"

"Two years now. Just parked my car."

"What apartment?"

"Three B."

"That's right under mine. Funny I never saw you in the building. Or in the garage."

"My job takes me on the road a great deal. Rarely spend nights here. Most weekends I'm away."

"How's your investigation going on the Dobbs story?"

"Well with the extraordinary cooperation I've received from Dancy Carter, Zack Zoltowsky and you, it's going nowhere fast."

"Have you seen Dancy Carter lately?"

"Phone conversation only. He's not very forthcoming."

"Does he have the number of your car phone or the public phone in the garage where you park?"

"I don't have a car phone, Miss Cabot. I don't even own a car."

"What were you doing in the garage?"

"Parking my car. A rental car. I'll be driving to Boston in the morning. Anybody there you want me to see? I'd be happy to oblige."

"Yes, I do. Your source at the FBI, or whomever is feeding you that drivel about Brian Dobbs' accident is really a murder."

"Will do. Good evening, Miss Cabot."

"Zack? It's Laura Dobbs. Did I catch you at an inconvenient time?"

"Laura. Hello. No it's not inconvenient. Forgive me for not calling you. I wanted to wait until things settled down."

"Zack, Brian hadn't touched a drop of whiskey in a year. Why would he fall off the wagon so far as to lose control of his car and smash into a wall?"

"I can't answer that, Laura, except to say that I've been off the sauce for a long time, but never get over the urge to have one for the road. Maybe Brian had that same urge, and it turned out to be one too many for the road."

"I don't buy it, Zack. He was very excited about being onto something really big. Why would he jeopardize that opportunity and go back to drinking?"

"Drunks, recovering or not, do not always make rational decisions."

"But he was back with you, he told me that the old team was going to reel in a big fish."

"All in his mind, Laura. He was exaggerating. All Brian had was a theory. Nothing more. Nothing solid. He pleaded with me to help and I agreed. Reluctantly, and only in a small way."

"Do you believe he got drunk all by himself? Do you believe it was an accident?"

"By himself? Who knows. Was it an accident? The M.E.'s report says yes. However, my gut instinct says maybe not. I have no concrete proof other than my gut."

"Me too, Zack."

"I realize that, but please don't dwell on maybes or you'll drive yourself nuts."

"Zack, I *am* driving myself nuts. What can we do? Is there anything you can do?"

"I'll dig around with some guys I still know at the Bureau to try to get to the bottom of this tragedy. If there is a bottom."

"Thank you, Zack. Although I really shouldn't care. Brian was seeing another woman and asked for a divorce. It's the children. I have to know for them. They deserve to remember their father as a good agent, not a drunk who died by his own hand. Find the truth, Zack. You're the one person I trust."

* * *

"Good afternoon, D.C. Are you listening? If so, I hope you recognize the soaring baritone of the great Billy Eckstine. That's the musical focus of today's 'DC ON THE AIR'...the unforgettable male singers of yesteryear.

"Oh by the way, I hope you recognize that this is Dancy Carter, DC if you may, on WTOP 1500 on your AM dial until 3 PM, where you hear the music you can't hear anyplace else. But you know that.

So for the next two hours stay tuned for Billy Eckstine, Joe Williams, Herb Jeffries, Arthur Prysock, Johnny Hartman, Jimmy Rushing, Fats Waller, Nat 'King' Cole, Der Bingle, Perry and Frank and others. We're gonna break for a commercial and then you're in for this musical treat with 'DC ON THE AIR,' on WTOP 1500 on your AM dial with the great male vocalists that are in every music lovers' Singers Hall of Fame.

Back in 60 seconds with Billy Eckstine and his marvelous version of Duke Ellington's classic 'Sophisticated Lady'."

* * *

   "Great opening, DC. People will get their money's worth today."
   "Sponsors will too, Zacko. Don't forget them. They pay the freight to keep the show on the air."
   "Almost forgot, DC. Our political guest today is Senator Dayton of Ohio."
   "The NRA lover, eh Zack?"
   "One and the same."
   "Well my trigger mouth is itching to shoot holes in his misguided point of view."
   "Remember the boss lady and the FCC, boss man."
   "How can I forget? Their ears will be burning, because I feel extra bold today. Cabot and the bureaucracy be damned."
   "Easy on the trigger, DC. Take it to the edge, but no more. We want to keep the show on the air."
   "Play the music, Zacko and leave the politics to me."
   "Ten seconds, Dancy."

   "DC, I got your message and glad you're on time this time. Just wish we had more light. Barely can see you."

"What did you learn from the M.E., Bob?"

"Bingo, DC. You were dead right."

"Not exactly appropriate language, Mr. Reporter."

"You're right. And you were right. There was an almost indiscernible trace of a sleep-inducing drug in the tox screen. If I hadn't pushed him to look for something, anything like that, he might never have found it. He's checking to see if that trace amount, mixed with alcohol, could have caused Dobbs to fall asleep at the wheel. And crash."

"What'll he do if he makes that finding?"

"Well, it's not exactly kosher, but he agreed to notify me first. What next, DC?"

"There is a right wing group committed to making White America Right America. It's called AFTRA. The Association For Tyranny and Rebellion in America. I know because I created the name."

"Kinda clever, DC."

"It has many, many important members of Congress, the military, business and the arts who have contributed untold millions and continue to do so. For the moment, however, who is not important. The money is."

"The root of all evil, DC. Especially for causes of this kind."

"Yes, but who has it and what's being done with it is the key. And as far as I can determine nothing has been done with those millions. A lot of smoke, but nothing tangible."

"Where is it going, DC?"

"I believe it's lining the pockets of the number one guy."

"Who's that?"

"I'm not going there yet, Bob. Just follow the money trail. One clue: It's an off-shore account. Find out who opened it. Once you get that piece of information, Mr. Big will come into focus. Then I'll give you the rest of the story."

"Off-shore where, Dancy?"

He was gone, as if he evaporated into thin air. Only a sheet of paper was left on the ground with two words on it: Grand Cayman. Woodstone smiled to himself. He had a good friend, a retired writer who lived in the Caymans. Follow the money trail the man said. Good suggestion Dancy Carter. You've set me on the right trail. The one paved with blood money. The murder of an FBI agent. The story is bigger than that, he thought.

"DC, the boss lady wants to see you ASAP, if not sooner. No excuses. She didn't say why."

"Oh, I know why, Zack. It's the FCC again, after I skewered that NRA hack. We'll hold our production meeting when I get back. I won't be long."

"Go easy on her, DC."

"Right."

* * *

"Dancy, thanks for coming."

"The message said urgent, and who am I to ignore an urgent message from the boss lady?"

"Kick the sarcasm, DC. We have to talk."

"I assume that's what I'm here for. Just know that my ears are wide open if we talk about the music I play, my intro or how I treat the sponsors. And definitely wide closed if by chance it's about the FCC. No sarcasm intended."

"Have you spoken to Bob Woodstone, or seen him in person lately, DC?"

"Er...yes. A few days ago...by phone. Why do you ask?"

"I'm having trouble with him about the Dobbs accident."

"Trouble? What kind?"

"No matter how I say it, I can't convince him that the FBI is way off base calling it a murder."

"It's not for you to convince him. Tell him to read the M.E.'s report."

"I did, but he says there's more to it. What's more, I know more."

"Look, Miss Cabot, this is old stuff. I don't have any advice for you, but I do have a production meeting in a few minutes. The show must go on. Are we through?"

"No. Woodstone and the Dobbs matter were just an excuse to get my tongue working properly. The real reason, the real urgent reason, is to discuss your run-in with the NRA hawk, Senator Dayton."

"Nice try, boss lady, but I'm out of here. We are through."

"Listen up, Mr. Carter. You took a real good shot at the Senator, and there wasn't a scintilla of fairness about your loathing of him and his position on the NRA."

"Scintilla? Nice word, Harvard lady. Now you listen up. In fact, turn up your hearing aid. If I'm going to be subjected to a speech about the FCC fairness rule, rule me out. And I will run, not walk, out your door."

"Dancy, please. I must. John Graham, the FCC radio coordinator, called about your segment. He's threatened censure for the station, for you. And that's the first step in recommending license withdrawal. Dancy, where are you going?"

"Out the door. The FCC doesn't mean squat to me, especially in this case. Where's their fairness doctrine when some dyed-in-the-wool gun lover is telling my audience that owning a gun is everyone's right and there should be no restrictions, AK47's and Uzis included. Those aren't guns for sport or to defend one's life and property. They are killing weapons. And that's exactly what's happening. Check the body count at the morgue."

"I read the papers, Dancy. Fairness, not venom, sir."

"Fairness my eye. I won't allow someone, anyone like him, to spew his evil opinions and get off so easily. The FCC can't condone a policy that censures me, but makes his rhetoric ok. Somebody has to stand up for the lawful citizens listening to the show who deplore the killings. Who have to bury their loved ones. The FCC and Dayton be damned."

"You must have a death wish, Carter. For your show, I mean. They can force us to take you off the air in a minute."

"Death wish? Strange choice of words."

"Sorry. That just slipped out."

"Yeah, sure. Drinking and driving, that's a death wish. Taking a radical gun-lover to task is a responsibility. And that's my job, because I have the power of the mike. See you around the mike. And please tell that bureaucratic hack that Dancy Carter is bigger than he is. Than the whole FCC. My listeners want me to fight for their rights. The FCC can do what they like."

"Can we have dinner, DC, and talk about this in a less formal business setting? Like my place."

"No more talking, any place. Especially yours. You have a way with a knife and fork and a goblet of wine that reduces my sense of reasoning to mere putty. Adios, boss lady."

"Dancy, you do have a death wish. The FCC. Your job. AFTRA. Dancy come back."

***

Bob Woodstone got to the garage five minutes past 5 PM thinking that he would find Carter waiting in the wings. He had to wait almost ten minutes before Carter appeared out of nowhere. Woodstone was certain he was hiding behind one of the columns using the darkness for his playing the spy game, adding another level of intrigue to their meeting.

"Hello, DC. Really playing this game right to the hilt. Right?"

"It's not a game, Bob. I have my reasons."

"Sorry. I didn't mean it that way. I apologize."

"What did you find out about the money?"

"Found loads of it. The money trail you suggested paid off. There's an account in a Grand Cayman bank with over fifty million dollars on deposit."

"Whew, I didn't expect that much. That's too much."

"What I didn't find was who owned the account. Oh, there was a name. A Jerome Bender. However, there is no Jerome Bender in Washington or Boston with any possibility of having fifty million dollars stashed away. It's obviously a fake name. Do you know who the real Jerome Bender is, DC?"

"No. the B is correct, but I never called him anything but Mr. B. I assume it should be easy to find out. Why not check what bank or banks here in the States initiated the wire transfers?"

"Did that. It was a dead end. This guy is very clever or he's got some big banking guys covering his tracks."

"Ok, here's another piece of the puzzle. There's a strong Boston connection of contributors. The B person might have an office there, since the telephone number I called was a Boston area code."

"Do you still have that number?"

"You bet. It's etched in my memory rolodex, but it's out of service."

"I've got connections at Boston telephone and might be able to find out who had that number. It's worth a shot. Let me have it."

"Forgot, Mr. Investigator, you have connections for everything. It was 617-556-0048,"

"Dancy, there's a larger question. Is this AFTRA a real political organization to do what you thought, or is it a front for a scam? You were an important cog in the operation. What's your take on it?"

"For a long time I believed that we were working towards changing America's racial and political face. Recently I started to feel that it was nothing more than a scheme to get people to shell out money. Finding out that there are fifty million big ones sitting out there, says scheme to me."

"Dancy, if Dobbs was murdered because he was getting close to the truth about AFTRA, and what you told me about being shunted to the background, is your life in danger?"

"Probably. That's why you have to find out everything and blow the lid off the group. Get the guy behind the scam. And keep me out of the story."

"I'm worried about you, DC."

"Don't. I have a plan to take care of myself."

"What next?"

"One more meeting and you should have everything you need to write the story, the whole story. Exposing AFTRA as nothing but a scam, and helping to put away, for a long time, a biggie who thought he could Ponzi people. People who really believed that White America was Right America. Write it, Bob. And soon. Time is running short."

"Is that your way of saying that time is running out on you? That the next 'accident' will be Dancy Carter?"

"Likely, Mr. Pulitzer."

"My God, DC, how can you be so cavalier about your life?"

"Get 'em, Bob, and I'll be less cavalier."

Woodstone was taken aback by Carter's attitude. He lit up a cigarette to calm himself. When he looked, Carter was gone. All he heard were footsteps. He raced to the spot where he had heard the noise, but there was no Carter. Only the stillness of an empty, darkened garage.

"Dancy! If you can hear me, watch your back."

***

"Good afternoon all you lucky, music-loving people out there in D.C. land. It's one o'clock, that time of the day to relax after lunch, at home or at work, and lend me your ears.

Oh, yeah, I'm DC, Dancy Carter, with 'DC ON THE AIR' till 3 PM on WTOP 1500 on your AM dial. The station that plays the music that melts away the tensions of the day. But you know that.

Why do I say you're lucky? That's because you're in for a treat. A multiple treat, so to speak. For the next two hours we'll be featuring many of the famous singing groups that harmonized their way into your hearts and minds.

The Incomparable Ink Spots. The Magnificent Mills Brothers. The Polyphonic Pied Pipers with Frank Sinatra. The Amiable Ames Brothers. The Mellow Mel-Tones led by Marvelous Mel Torme. And many others. That swinging sound you hear in the background is the Mills Brothers with their classic version of 'IT'S ONLY A PAPER MOON.'

Hit the volume Mr. Producer."

* * *

"What a sound. What harmony. And for those of you who just tuned in that was the Brothers Mills and I'm DC, Dancy Carter, with 'DC ON THE AIR' on WTOP 1500 on your AM dial.

Before we continue folks, I want to take a few minutes to express my gratitude to all you people who tune in every day. Who have made us the number 1 show in D.C. Without you, DC would be just another DJ. Thanks for writing and calling in the music you want me to play. The music I love to play for you. It's been a privilege. So from the bottom of my heart, I thank you. Keep those cards and calls coming.

Also thanks for your timely, informed questions during our call-in segment. I take a great deal of pleasure in bursting the inflated balloons of the politicians who voice their opinions...usually on the wrong side of the issues that affect your life. I know this is true because you tell me it's true, even though the bureaucrats at the FCC don't see eye-to-eye with me. They can't win. You won't let them. Got that off my chest, folks. Thanks for indulging me.

Now back to the music and the Incomparable Ink Spots with 'IT'S A SIN TO TELL A LIE'."

* * *

"DC, what was that all about? Your swan song? Are you bidding farewell to 'DC ON THE AIR'?"

"I'm tired Zack, physically and emotionally. Everyone wants a piece of me. All the accusations. The FBI intimating that I had something to do with Dobbs' death. Friends, too. Bob Woodstone snooping around.

Even my private life is under scrutiny. The FCC busting my chops after every interview. Cabot trying to rein me in."

"I know. That's a lot on your plate."

"It's getting more difficult every day to get up, much less get up for the show with that many distractions. It's not fun anymore."

"Is that a yes, DC?"

"A definite maybe, maybe. It has entered my mind."

"DC, you're not a quitter. You've never walked away from a fight or a challenge."

"It's more difficult, Zack."

"Difficult, maybe. Impossible no. The FBI can't link you up with Dobbs' death. I know that for sure."

"That doesn't mean they won't press it."

"And the FCC. DC, they're just a pimple on the ass of an elephant. It's there but you can barely see it."

"Yeah, but it's like a boil on mine."

"Let's be realistic, Dancy. Money talks in radio land, and the station bigwigs would never take you off the air. The loss of revenue would be staggering."

"Marty Martin is a good DJ and could keep it coming in, Zack."

"No way. The station's ratings would plummet without Dancy Carter, and advertisers would pull out immediately. Revenue would drop like the fall leaves. Besides that, your audience wants their DC. They're loyal to a fault. They won't accept anyone else."

"That's nice of you to say."

"I mean every word of it, DC. And speaking for Zacko, I know you didn't have a thing to do with Dobbs' death. It was a tragic accident."

"Why does the Bureau keep saying otherwise?"

"Covering their bureaucratic asses. They always protect the reputation of their agents. A drunken agent crashing into a wall is not good for his reputation, and not good for the Bureau's image. Publicly calling it murder gets that bad image off the hook."

"The gout doesn't work, right Zack?"

"That's the DC I believe in. Funning in the face of a tough situation."

"Yeah, Zack, funning with tears in my eyes."

"The Bureau has no proof, DC. In the end they'll admit it was an accident. They can't change the M.E.'s report. He's not in bed with the Bureau."

"Thanks for that, Zacko. A friend is a friend. I don't know what the future holds for me. Right now things are spiraling out of control and I'm caught in the updraft."

"Hang tight, DC."

"We'll have to see, Zacko. We'll have to see."

"Thirty seconds, DC."

"Play the second cut of the Ink Spots."

"Want to do an intro?"

"Music, Mr. Producer. Enough talking for now."

"Dancy, it's Jennifer. Glad I caught you before you left. Are you still in that funny, spaced-out mode when I bumped into you at Watergate?"

"Neither, Miss Cabot. Just tired."

"Stop calling me Miss Cabot."

"Alright, Miss Jennifer Cabot. What do you want? Make it quick, I have an appointment."

"Don't brush me off, Dancy Carter. What the heck was that 'it's a privilege' bit you were handing out?"

"Just letting my loyal listeners know what I think of them, and how much I appreciate their tuning in."

"That's a crock, Mr. C., and you know it. You know what I think? That the irrepressible, irresponsible, irreplaceable music man is throwing in the towel. Am I getting close?"

"Everything but the irreplaceable."

"No time for funning, lover. Is the FCC really getting to you? If so, you got to them first. You really blistered them enough to raise their bureaucratic blood pressure to the boiling point."

"Just telling it like it is."

"Well, if that was the reason for your 'it's a privilege' but don't give it a second thought."

"Oh, dear lady, for sure I won't."

"I can handle them. I can plead that you were temporarily insane. That you were drinking heavily…coffee, that is, and were wired beyond control."

"Good thinking. Good for you, I might add. You've made a perfect case to take me off the air."

"That's not what I was trying to say."

"Seriously, Jen. I am thinking of turning in my microphone. It's not just one thing. I'm tired and disillusioned."

"Take some time off. Take a cruise. I'll have Marty Martin fill in."

"That's not it. Friends and foes pointing fingers, blaming me for Dobbs' death. Woodstone in my face. The FBI on my ass. And the clincher: The top man in AFTRA thinking I'm a liability. Too visible and a threat to AFTRA."

"Don't believe a word of it."

"Can you imagine that, Dancy Carter too visible. A liability. I thought I was the biggest asset he had."

"You are. Whatever he had to do with Dobbs' accident, he's making you the scapegoat. He knows violence is not what you advocate, and would speak out against it."

"Damn right I would."

"Don't throw away your career for him."

"Nothing is clear now. It's all out of focus. However, you and the station will not be hung out to dry. I'll stay with 'DC ON THE AIR' for awhile till I sort it all out. Your bottom line won't suffer."

"For God's sake, Dancy, do you think so little of me that you believe that's what I'm talking about? What I care about, you big lug, is you."

"Do I get a sense that love with a commoner is hidden between the lines?"

"Not hidden. Out in the open. My worry is your fragile state of mind. That the egotistical, arrogant, usually optimistic man I love and adore is breaking into little pieces right before my eyes."

"At least one thing is a positive."

"I've laid myself bare to you, DC, level with me. What is really troubling you?"

"All the things I mentioned before are troubling to a degree, but not like AFTRA. It's become an albatross around my neck. The man says I'm a liability. Imagine the DC man having to live with the idea of being a liability? Do you believe I'm a liability, Jen?"

"Not for one second, but you are becoming a basket case. I told you a long time ago to get out. You jumped into waters that were too deep for you to swim."

"Funny you should say that. That's what he told me."

"Just get out, now. Your listeners will understand and forgive you for being up front with them. No equivocation. Tell them the truth."

"The truth, after all the lies?"

"Anyone is entitled to make a mistake. Tell them you made a whopper. They'll believe you were duped. Sell it to them, DC. Sell it like you sell them on your music and the products you ask them to buy."

"Too late, too little, Boston lady. I'm not really breaking apart. Troubled, yeah, but holding up. Thanks for caring so deeply, though."

"Let's put all this behind us, DC. Have dinner at my place tonight. Pizza, Petrus and petting will make things better. How does that grab you?"

"Nice try, Jen. Better, yes, but disappear, no. Have to go. Hope you can keep the FCC off your back. Speak to you again."

Jennifer just stared at the phone for a long time after he hung up. He's up to something, she thought. Something that smells trouble. Carter is at Watergate, no reason to be there. Woodstone is at Watergate, contrived reason to be there. Hardly coincidental. Then the swan song speech on the air. That's not the Carter I know. The Carter everybody knows. The DC man of D.C. He's hurting badly was all she could think of. She wondered what it meant. What was he going to do next? Maybe Zack had a clue.

"Dancy, Bob Woodstone. Glad I caught you."
"Just leaving, Bob, what's up?"

"A heads up for you, my friend. All the pieces are in place. The puzzled is finished and I'm writing the story as we speak."

"Every piece, Bob?"

"We got them, DC. The facts have been confirmed by three sources."

"Wonderful. When do you break the story?"

"Just as soon as our legal eagles say go and the Publisher puts her stamp of approval on it. I'd say in three days."

"Everything, Bob. Really everything?"

"Yes, sir, from the inception of AFTRA by the infamous Mr. B., his identity, the politicians who were up to their necks in a plot to change the face of America to pure white, the contributors who felt the same way or believed that's what AFTRA was all about, the money offshore, and last but not least, the murder of FBI agent Brian Dobbs."

"That took a lot of digging, Mr. Woodstone."

"Yeah, DC, but you provided the shove. And the deeper I dug, the more I uncovered. It was all unbelievable. This falls short of being Watergate 2, only because a President won't have to resign. Some pols will."

"You name them all?"

"Every single one except Dancy Carter."

"I was told that names were not on any record."

"You were told a big fib, DC. The illustrious, soon-to-be-in-prison leader, Mr. William Claymore Bagwell, the founder of Bagwell Industries, and a pillar of the communities of Charleston, South Carolina and Boston, Massachusetts, kept copious records of each AFTRA member's contributions. Every dollar, every name."

"My God, you would think that a smart con man would never leave a paper trail like that."

"It was by design, DC. This was the sword he held over everyone's head if they got out of line. One wrong step and he would let that person know his name was on the record."

"That wouldn't keep him from being involved."

"Right. He wasn't smart there either. I guess he felt that one's public exposure as a radical, right wing racist would be his hole card."

"What about the contributors? Will they be brought up on charges? Jail time, that is."

"Maybe not. My Justice Department source says it isn't a crime to contribute money to any organization unless they know the money was to be used for illegal activities, they deducted it as a contribution on their income tax form and the group was not a tax exempt entity, or participated in an illegal activity for the group."

"So the Cabots and friends are off the hook."

"Probably, as long as all they did was pony up money."

"Even though they wanted to change America? The Constitution?"

"Wanting and doing are two different things."

"Congratulations are in order, Bob. You did a hell of a job."

"Most of the credit goes to you, DC. I was floundering around with a non-story until you pointed me in the right direction."

"Looks like another Pulitzer for the Woodstone trophy room."

"If so, DC, half the trophy and half the cash award belong to you."

"Forget it. We made a pact, remember? Never, ever to reveal me as your source. Right?"

"I never reveal a source. Your secret is safe. Don't know why you want it that way, though. I'm sure you're aware, DC, that when the story breaks, all the people who thought you were involved will know you were."

"Painfully aware."

"What will you do then?"

"Won't have to do a thing, because I'll be long gone before it hits the fan."

"Long gone or gone long?"

"Take your pick. If you hear that I've disappeared under strange circumstances or that foul play is suggested, just know that I worked it out."

"I hope it's of your doing, DC."

"Either way, Bob, it doesn't change our agreement about being your source."

"Where will you go, Dancy? You're too much of a celebrity just to move to another city."

"You don't want to know, my friend. Not revealing me as your source is one thing, you can't be forced to reveal something you don't know. Write the good words, Bob, and make sure the bad guys are put away."

"One final question, DC. Why did you blow the whistle on a cause you fervently believed in? Not to mention destroying your celebrity status in Washington?"

"I don't have a simple answer. Many things, Bob, many complex things. Dobbs' murder started a chain reaction. Murder was beyond the scope of my involvement in AFTRA.

The deception. Not being true to fighting for the rights of people who were left behind in the political process started to bug me."

"I'm amazed, DC, that you could juggle both sides without being totally confused."

"More importantly, I found myself fighting a latent sort of bigotry that crept up on me when I wasn't looking. Bagwell read me on all of this and sold me that White America is Right America."

"Con men can do it. They smell the weaknesses."

"I began to dislike Dancy Carter for deluding friends, my loyal radio audience who believed the sun rose and set on me. Doubt crept in and it began to eat me up."

"That's a heavy burden to carry around, DC."

"More than that. My instincts told me there was something fishy about what he was telling me and not telling me. Nothing was happening politically. There was no accounting of the money."

"Wasn't it all to be secret, DC? Nothing on paper or easy to trace."

"True, but why was all the money in an off-shore bank? How can you fund things on shore when the money is off-shore? I came to the conclusion that B. was running a scam. The cause was a sham. I was a pawn. That's when I said Bob Woodstone can make the scam public."

"Why not stay and face the music, DC? You are the man in D.C. Your friends, your radio audience, even the media will be on your side. I will help by revealing that you were the source that brought down Bagwell and AFTRA."

"Don't give that idea a second thought. You promised. The first idea has been suggested many times before, but I can't pull off another deception to save my career and reputation."

"We can work it out, Dancy."

"No, Bob, the guilt would ultimately consume me. Believe me, I've thought about it a long time. It's best I take a ride to somewhere, and let anyone, everyone think I'm dead."

"That seems like an awfully high price to pay, DC."

"Not the way I see it. It's a small price to pay for not living up to what real people thought about me."

"I don't agree, but I won't try and stop you. Thanks for the story."

"Good luck with it, Bob. Just get it into print quickly. And thanks for the heads-up."

"Good luck to you, DC, whatever you do."

"Don't worry, I'll come out of this alive. No matter that the D.C. world will presume that DC is dead."

THREE DAYS LATER

The headline on the front page of the Washington Post screamed out in big block letters:

CEO INDICTED: MURDER. FRAUD. SCAM.

Byline Bob Woodstone

The arrest and indictment by Federal officials of William Claymore Bagwell, CEO of a Fortune 500 company, Bagwell Industries of Charleston South Carolina and Boston, Massachusetts, broke the back of a right wing organization called AFTRA (The Association for Tyranny and Rebellion in America).

This reporter, with information provided by an anonymous source, discovered that AFTRA was a scam of Ponzi proportions. Mr. Bagwell collected over 50 million dollars from high profile people in public and private life to supposedly make White America Right America.

They were deluded into believing that AFTRA would be using this money to influence and infiltrate Congressional committees, introduce legislation to promote its right wing agenda, even rewriting the Constitution to literally create a society with one color, white, reaping the benefits. The benefits, however, would only accrue to Mr. Bagwell. 50 Million Dollars worth. AFTRA was founded over two years ago, yet never registered with the IRS as a charitable organization or political one. In fact, there's no record of any kind that it even existed. They had no headquarters, no phone listing, no staff. It was the personal money machine of Mr. Bagwell.

My anonymous source also revealed to this reporter that the 50 million dollars were deposited in an off-shore bank. Further digging revealed that the money was in a bank in the Grand Cayman Islands under the name of Jerome Bender. Jerome Bender, in fact, was William Claymore Bagwell.

This scam took on more serious consequences when my source revealed that an FBI agent, Brian Dobbs, who died in a car accident, was actually murdered. Agent Dobbs was actively investigating AFTRA, and was close to an arrest of Mr. Bagwell, when he mysteriously crashed into a wall while supposedly driving drunk. It was declared an accidental death. With additional information from my source, further examination of the body and the toxicology report by the ME revealed an almost undecipherable drug in the bloodstream that caused the agent to fall asleep at the wheel and crash. The accident finding was officially changed to murder. Other evidence uncovered proof that Mr. Bagwell ordered the gang-like hit.

Further digging by this reporter unearthed the list of contributors to AFTRA that was stored away, along with the 50 million dollars, all in cash, in that same vault. The list was Bagwell's ace in the hole if any contributor got out of linc. In reality it was an extortion ace.

Mr. Bagwell surrendered to FBI agents in his Boston office late last night, and will be arraigned as you read this article. Bagwell declined to make a statement, but his attorney said he is innocent of all charges.

In my follow up articles, I will name names of the prominent contributors and many more details of this sordid story. Details that resemble the Watergate fiasco because of the high profile Washington people involved.

"Jennifer, Miss Cabot, have you read Woodstone's article in the Post? I can't believe it. Dobbs was telling the truth and was murdered for it."

"Hard to miss Zack. Ask Dancy to see me when he comes in."

"Do you think he was part of this AFTRA scam?"

"Not the scam itself, but he was the Washington front man."

"Are you sure?"

"About the scam, absolutely. Involvement with AFTRA, yes. I was involved as well. Contributed money to help change things in America."

"Oh my God, Dancy and you. Then I was right about DC and Dobbs' murder. He murdered him."

"No, Zack, he had nothing to do with that. Dancy was against violence and had no idea that Bagwell ordered Dobbs to be killed."

"Do you think he's Woodstone's anonymous source?"

"Possibly. He's been acting very strange lately. Bumped into him coming out of my Watergate garage dressed like a spy. Minutes later Woodstone came out of the same garage offering up a very lame reason. Coincidence? I don't think so."

"Jen, that's Deep Throat déjà vu."

"Yep, my thoughts exactly. Then there was his 'it's a privilege' bit on the air. Sounded like a farewell speech to me."

"He just about admitted that to me, Jen."

"However, the clincher was when he told me the head man considered him a liability to AFTRA, and to stop doing any more work for him. This really upset him."

"Upset enough to blow the whistle with Woodstone?"

"I think so, but let's not jump to any conclusions. I'll ask him when he comes in."

"Will he tell us?"

"Maybe not you, but I hope he would confide in me."

Jennifer ran into Zack's office and with panic in her voice asked, "Where's DC? He's on in 30 minutes."

"I don't know, Jen. I called the apartment. No answer. The answering machine did not pick up, either. Couldn't reach him on his cell. I don't know where he is or what to think."

"DC has never missed a show, Zack. I'm worried."

"Me too. Something doesn't smell right."

"Are the CDs set up for today's show?"

"Ready to go. Just need the man to work his cues for the intro."

"I'm putting Marty Martin behind the mike. Work with him to start, then Jim Brant will take over for you."

"What'll we do then, Jen?"

"Call the hospitals. Check the morgue."

"The morgue? Do you think he's dead?"

"I don't know what to think. He's MIA. Let's check everywhere."

"Why don't we bring in the police, Jen?"

"Right I didn't think of that. Do that first and tell them to meet us at Dancy's apartment in an hour."

The doorman said that Mr. Carter came home after 9 PM and never came down again, but could go out by using the back entrance.

Jennifer and Zack had the super open the door to his apartment. There was an eerie silence when they stepped into the foyer.

"He can't be far away, Jen. His wallet has lots of cash and his credit cards. House and car keys are here. Coffee machine is set up in the kitchen. Nothing seems to be missing."

"Looks like he didn't sleep in his bed, Zack, unless he made it up before stepping out. Clothes are all here, too. Luggage is in the closet."

"Nothing missing in the bathroom, Jen. Razor, shaving cream, comb and brush. Toothpaste and Waterpik."

"So Zack, everything is here. Nothing missing except DC. Where the hell is he? Let's hang around for awhile. Hopefully he'll be back shortly."

"Where are the police, Jen? They should have been here a half hour ago."

At that moment, a burly, beer-barreled man strolled into the apartment, a big cigar in his mouth.

"Oh, hi. You are the police, I hope?" said Jennifer. "Glad you could make it."

"Are you Jennifer Cabot?"

"In person. And your name, sir?"

"Detective Sergeant Mack Williams."

"Thanks for coming, detective. As you can see, Mr. Carter is not here. All his personal items are. I suggest you call in a Missing Person Alert immediately."

"Sorry Miss Cabot, I cannot do that yet. Mr. Carter is probably out jogging or having lunch someplace."

"Jogging? He doesn't jog. He hates exercise. And he doesn't have lunch any place but at the radio station."

"It don't matter, lady. We have to wait 24 hours before making a call that Mr. Carter is missing. That's procedure."

"Procedure? Listen up, detective. We have a very important celebrity missing and probably in real danger. In 24 hours he could be dead. And you and your procedure will be responsible."

"Push all you want, lady, but procedure is procedure."

"Alright, Sergeant, if you won't make the call, I will. To your Captain. He's a very good friend of Carter and me. We'll see about your procedure.

"Captain James! Jennifer Cabot. I've got a procedure problem with one of your detectives that needs your immediate attention."

"Like what, Jennifer?"

"Dancy Carter is missing. He didn't make his show today, and you know that's something he has never done before. He didn't call in sick or anything."

"Missing? Just the show, or missing period?"

"Missing. Everything he owns is in his place, but he's not. There are things happening in his life that place him in grave danger."

"How can I help?"

"Order a missing person alert now. Your Detective Williams says procedure calls for you to wait 24 hours before an alert can be issued. It can't wait."

"Where are you now, Jennifer?"

"At DC's apartment."

"Sit tight. I'll be there ASAP with a forensic team and my best detectives to search the area. We'll check train stations, bus depots, airports, every place possible. I'll issue the alert immediately. Don't worry, Jennifer, we'll find him."

"Thanks, Chief."

"Put Sergeant Williams on."

For the next twelve hours, the Washington police were in a full search mode. Forensic experts checked DC's computer files, phone records, appointment book, bank records, anything that might be a clue to his whereabouts.

Detectives spread out around the city, checking informants and places Carter frequented. Regular blue coat officers canvassed neighbors, surrounding buildings, local parks, movie theaters and restaurants. They came up empty. Not a hint of where he might have been since 9 PM last night. Dancy Carter, DC, a face as well known in Washington, D.C. as the President, had vanished into thin air.

That next morning, Bob Woodstone's second article on the AFTRA exposé ran on the front page of the Washington Post, but was eclipsed by blaring headlines and a two-column story of the mysterious disappearance of Washington's popular music man, Dancy Carter.

DC didn't have to be on the air to be the biggest story in D.C.

For the next 48 hours there was an all-out search for Dancy Carter. Posters were put up all around the D.C. area and its environs. Students from many of the colleges worked in teams to hopefully find a clue about his whereabouts. WTOP ran announcements every half hour offering a $50,000 reward for any information. Anonymity would be honored. The other radio and television stations also ran continuous announcements. Hundreds of people called in with DC sightings. He was seen at a bowling alley, a movie theater, having dinner at Dukes, boarding a plane at Ronald Reagan airport, a Greyhound bus to Boston, casually eating an ice cream cone on a bench in the park. None of these frivolous sightings proved anything but frivolous. Dancy Carter simply seemed to vanish off the face of the Earth.

In Zack Zoltowski's opinion, with Brian Dobbs' murder fresh in his mind, DC was probably six feet under the earth.

Jennifer and Zack made impassioned pleas on radio, TV and news conferences all day long. They appealed particularly to Carter's loyal audience on WTOP to come forth with any information, no matter how insignificant. Nothing came from their pleas and prayers. Every time the phone rang at the stations their hopes rose, only to be dashed, shattered by some kook with a wild theory of what happened to Dancy Carter. Jennifer Cabot, with panic slowly building and fearful for DC's life, hired Washington's most prestigious private security firm to work independently of the police. They looked overseas as well. She was convinced that the police were incompetent, maybe not even taking his disappearance seriously.

She desperately needed to be directly involved, and in control. This included a huge fee to WDC Investigations, with the promise of an equally large bonus, to go all out in their search. Two days later, although the DC story still commanded attention, Bob Woodstone's third and final article on AFTRASCAM ran, giving more sordid details and naming more of the contributors.

It created shock waves in the D.C. community when people learned that some of the most prominent names in politics, the military, society circles, the corporate world, academia and the entertainment business were on the list.

The society world in particular was rocked when it was uncovered that Jennifer Cabot, her mother Carolyn, brother John and other Boston socialites were on the list. Boston's right wing was well represented.

The U.S. Attorney's office issued a statement saying that most of the people named in Woodstone's articles would not be charged with a crime. They had every right to support AFTRA. If, however, any evidence surfaced that they knew illegal activities were being subsidized by them, they would prosecute to the fullest extent of the law.

The IRS took a different, more aggressive position. They would be auditing the tax returns of all those listed, to determine if anyone declared his contribution as a charitable tax deduction.

Bob Woodstone in a television interview made it clear that being charged or not, shame would follow those who supported an agenda designed to subvert the Constitution and the democratic process...and who advocated racial bias.

He also indicated rather sarcastically that William Claymore Bagwell, the architect of AFTRASCAM and the one who allegedly ordered the murder of an FBI agent, would be exchanging his expensive pin-striped suits for prison stripes. Bagwell would have to forfeit the $50 million he scammed, as well as pay millions in penalties to the government. * * *

Days after the story broke, Jennifer Cabot resigned her position at the station, left the country and rented a villa in the South of France.

Carolyn Cabot continued her reign as Queen of Boston society, virtually thumbing her nose at the liberal activists thirsting for her blood. She made it perfectly clear that her world did not have to apologize for beliefs that White America was Right America.

Weeks later, many of the other prominent people named in the Woodstone exposé left Washington for faraway places, embarrassed and humiliated. Not only because of their right wing advocacy, but by being scammed by a man they called a friend, a man they all looked up to.

Zack Zoltowski, although in great mental pain over Dobbs' murder and overwhelmed by Dancy Carter's deception and then disappearance, and a dreaded sense that he was dead, stayed on as the producer. He felt he had an obligation to Carter's loyal and adoring listeners. The show was renamed 'MMM ON THE AIR' with Marty Matt Martin as the DJ. Martin played the same kind of music. However, two months later, with ratings falling like the winter thermometer and advertisers cancelling in droves, Zack resigned and moved to a small town in Vermont.

Six months later, when all the hoopla ran its course, the Washington, D.C. Police Chief announced that the Dancy Carter investigation was being terminated.

That Mr. Carter was officially declared dead, probably a victim of foul play. However, the case would remain in the cold case file, technically still open, since there was no statute of limitations on murder.

ONE YEAR LATER

When the phone rang, Zack Zoltowski was surprised to hear a very familiar voice.

"Zack, I'm back."

"Jennifer? Jennifer Cabot? Is that really you? How did you ever track me down?"

"The CEO of WDC owed me a favor for not finding Dancy."

"Oh, it's good to hear your voice. Where did you go? How are you? And what have you been doing, Jen?"

"Running, Zack. Running all around Europe. France. Italy. Germany. Trying to forget. Feeling guilty as all hell that I didn't push harder to get Dancy to get out of AFTRA. Even now, I hate to say that word. I'm ok now and made peace with myself."

"I hated everything, too. Dancy and his deception, Dobbs for drawing me into his ill-fated venture, the station, even the music I loved. It wasn't easy at first, but slowly but surely I found peace."

"Speaking of Dancy, is there anything new? Any sign that he may still be alive?"

"Well, Jen, I've been away from Washington for quite some time and have been out of the loop. There's no sign at all whether he's dead or alive. However, last I heard the case has been closed. Dancy has been officially declared dead."

"I can't believe it Zack. It's so unreal. One year ago we were at the top of the music world and now there is no bottom."

"Same for me, Jen. It's been difficult. A lot of sleepless nights, a lot of what ifs. I felt badly for his loyal listeners that hung on his every word. Lionized him."

"I know how you felt. I loved that guy. His talent. His passion. His humor. Even his misguided involvement with AFTRA. He was a paradox. A man who led two lives with seemingly no problem. AFTRA was important to him, but he never gave up fighting for his people about issues that affected them, that he could influence."

"He certainly was a paradox, Jen."

"He took on the FCC with a vengeance, even though it might jeopardize his job. Not to mention, my job, and his relationship with me. Talk about sleep. I don't know how he slept at night."

"My hate has long been dissipated, Jen. Thinking back, he was 'funning' most of the time, and fun to be with. His knowledge of the music he played was simply amazing. The music came alive with DC's hands on the control. I came alive. The show became the most important thing in my life."

"Amen to that, Zack."

"I only hope, Jen, he's playing that good stuff up there, wherever, for a brand new audience."

"That would be nice. Got to run. Goodbye, Zack, and good luck."

"Goodbye, Jen. Good luck to you, and I hope you continue to have peace of mind.

TWO YEARS LATER—PORT HARDY, BRITISH COLUMBIA

"A hearty good morning to all you good folks in Port Hardy, B.C. It's your old music man BC, Blaney Crater with 'BC ON THE AIR' on CDFNI, 1240 on your AM Dial, Monday thru Friday 10 AM to 12 Noon.

"The weather outside is just a bit nippy. 42 degrees nippy. No matter, 'cause if you stay real close to your music box, BC will warm the cockles of your heart. Yes, sir. We have a musical treat lined up for you this morning on your favorite show, on your favorite music station.

Like what you ask? Glad you did. How about the best in Jumpin' Jazz with Ella, Billie, Nat Cole, the Count…Bluesy Blues with Satchmo, Bessie Smith, Jimmy Rushing and the Golden Oldies of the big bands with Dorsey, Goodman, Miller and Woody Herman and the Thundering Herd.

The good stuff, folks, only the way BC can bring it to you.

But you know that."

ABOUT THE AUTHOR

This is L.C. Goldman's third published novel, on the heels of his recently critically acclaimed "A BIG HIT IN PELICAN BAY."

His knowledge and passion for music, jazz in particular, is evident in "FROM LEFT TO RIGHT," an intriguing story of music, murder and mystery.

Using the skills he honed as an advertising executive for over 40 years supervising major consumer names such as: Ralph Lauren, Polo and Chaps colognes, Seagram, Perrier Jouet Champagne, the Concorde (SST), Yves St. Laurent and Armitron Watches, L.C. brings to life a smooth-talking radio disc jockey with a vast musical background, who leads a double political life.

Dancy Carter, DC to the Washington, D.C. listening audience, is an unforgettable character with more celebrity than the President of the United States.

L.C. enjoys his retirement living in Pelican Bay in Naples, Florida, tooling around town in his BMW Z4, writing novels, playing golf and being involved in community activities.

Printed in the United States
201443BV00002B/349-381/P